T0065193

THE
CULMINATORS

THE CULMINATORS

A bounty hunting, romance, and entrepreneur series, Book 9

Richard M Beloin MD

To order additional copies of this book, contact:
Xlibris
844-714-8691
www.Xlibris.com
Orders@Xlibris.com
852858

CONTENTS

DEDICATION

This book is dedicated to my good friend, Larry. He knows what it's like to work as a lumberjack and operate lumber saws.

CHAPTER 1

The Early Days

Ray 'Coop' Cooper, age 20, had been a bounty hunter for two years. He had been chosen by Enos Straus who needed a shootist to complement his shotgun skills. After two years of training on the job, Ray had no choice but to go solo when Enos developed a heart condition and had to retire. After a couple of capers, which nearly did him in without a backup, Ray was considering an early retirement.

His current hunt involved days on the trail from Amarillo, Texas in pursuit of the Simpson Gang who had robbed the Amarillo Wells Fargo Bank of $40,000. Finally arriving in New Braunfels, he found their headquarters in an abandoned trapper's cabin two miles out of town.

Being alone, Ray devised a way to disable the half dozen outlaws, without risking his own life. Having learned the proper handling of dynamite, he decided to demolish the cabin while the outlaws were inside and likely drunk and sleeping. Around 3AM under a full moon, Ray pushed two long fused dynamite sticks under the block elevated cabin. Rushing to a large pine tree with ear plugs, he fired a shotgun buckshot round into the front window just as the fuse was nearly burnt out. The gun blast woke everyone up about 30 seconds ahead of the devastation.

Ray was fifty yards away, behind a huge pine tree, and with extra earmuffs, as the dynamite exploded. The entire cabin lifted up as floorboards and outlaws were blown out of windows and doors. Two walls had collapsed outward and the roof was held up by two precarious walls. Outlaws were crawling out of the cabin with nosebleeds, bleeding ears, broken bones, and many lacerations and bruises. Two outlaws were dead with deformed skulls and most of the others were vomiting or unable to stand. It took Ray hours to find the saddlebags full of cash and load the disabled and dead outlaws onto their horses.

By daylight, Ray was leading a caravan of dead and near comatose outlaws. As they arrived at Sheriff Dolan's office, he was greeted by deputy Crandall, who saw the morbid bunch and decided to get the sheriff. The sheriff came out of his office as he recognized Ray. "Well Coop,

I see you're still at it, so tell me who you have today." "The Simpson Gang out of Amarillo and here is the heisted loot of $40,000 for Wells Fargo minus my 10% finder's fee of $4,000." "These outlaws have bounties on their heads and we'll have to settle later." As the deputy was escorting four into the jail, two were being sent to the undertaker. Ray was just about to sit down and enjoy a fresh cup of coffee with the sheriff when several gunshots were heard.

Sheriff Dolan jumped up and said, "those shots are coming from our Wells Fargo branch—three blocks from here." That was enough info as all three men took off on a dead run. Arriving at the bank, a crowd was already gathering. The lawmen went right into the bank while Ray stood at the back of the gathered crowd. Without realizing who was standing next to him, Ray suddenly saw a huge brown dog pawing his left leg. Ray was surprised but realized that the dog was smelling a piece of jerky in his rear pocket. After rubbing his head and ears, he offered the dog the piece of jerky. To his surprise, he heard a lady's voice say, "well you must have some strange scent because half-wolf Browny never befriends strangers." "Well Ma'am, that's because I love all animals." As he spoke the last word, he turned to face that lady's voice.

Next to him was a sight he would never forget. It was a 6-foot-tall slim gal with bright shining brown hair fluffed up to her shoulders, with full female attributes to include full bosom, round bottom, and all the curves that go to outline a voluptuous woman. Not seeing a ring on her finger he said, "oh sorry Miss, I didn't see you before I called you Ma'am." The gal answered, "so you're the famous Coop—an ethical bounty hunter that historically precedes you. My name is Elle Belton, 'E-double L-E,' and you've already met my guard dog, Browny."

"Yes Miss, my full name is Ray Cooper, but I prefer being called Ray—that's Ra with a 'Y.' Ray by instinct stepped up and handed the gal his hand. She responded as both seemed to linger. Browny came over to certify that he was the gal's private bodyguard as he pushed his way between her legs. To carry a conversation he said, "do you know what happened in there?" "Yes, there was a bank robbery by the Hollister gang, a cashier was killed when President Willis refused to open the vault, and after he opened it he was pistol whipped. Doc Summers is now attending him." "How much was taken?" "$35,000 plus change as it was the payroll week for the entire ranching community."

Ray was going to follow up with another question when the sheriff came out and said, "I want a twelve-man posse ready to meet here in 15 minutes—men able to ride hard and shoot to kill. We're going to run this gang down once and for all." Speaking to himself he said, *"oh boy, that is not good. This gang is known to hold up down the road and pull a lethal ambush."* Despite the sheriff rushing to get his gear and horse, he did manage to warn the sheriff.

Standing by the boardwalk, he and the young gal watched the posse take off with a bunch of town dandies. Elle could not resist and said, "you don't think they will all come back, do you?" "No Miss, half will be across their saddle and a couple will have serious gunshot wounds." "So what are you going to do about it?" "I am going after them, for that is what I do—as dangerous as it is!" "But Mister, you are alone, the outlaws are close to a half-dozen, and you don't even have a backup shooter." "It is what it is," as he started to walk away.

Elle raised her voice as she said, "let Browny and me come along. I am very deadly with my modified coach shotgun plus Browny can disable or kill any attacker. Let us be your backup!" "Wow, I certainly appreciate the offer and I am sure you and Browny have much sand. Yet I cannot risk a woman's life by placing her in danger— for these outlaws want only one thing, to kill anyone who wants to arrest them."

Elle said nothing more but thought, *"now there goes a man with a work ethic and respect for human life. Well, he is going to find out that this woman can hold her own and is willing to put any outlaw down that is trying to kill him or me or Browny!"*

*

Ray politely doffed his hat and said goodbye to the gal named Elle. Arriving at Zeke's General Store, he purchased vittles for the trail and a change of clothes. Stepping outside, that gorgeous brown-haired gal with a friendly wolfdog, was sitting on a boardwalk bench. Loading his goods onto the extra-large saddlebags, he then addressed the waiting lady. "Well Miss, when I return, I would love to see you and learn your story to the present. Could I call on you, Elle, E-double L-E. "You may, Ra with a Y—if you ever return going after six killers without a backup?" "Well, let me tell you a secret, 'some people are not meant to die young, heh?'" Elle selected her response by saying, "precautionary measures can enable that fatalistic attitude to come to fruition, heh?" Ray nodded and stepped into the stirrup and mounted while doffing his hat for the second time today.

As soon as Ray was out of sight, she got on her horse and headed home at a full trot. Browny kept up and was on her house's front porch as she tied the reins to the railing. Inside she exchanged her revolver for her dad's 41 long colt with hot loads, and picked up her tricked 12-gauge double barrel shotgun with the extra hot OO Buckshot loads. With some extra clothes and some rain gear, she took off with Browny at her side. On the trail, she stopped to see one of her neighbors and arranged for him to feed and water the chickens, for the eggs he would gather, until her return.

Meanwhile, Ray was following the posse tracks when all of a sudden, the sheriff followed by a defeated posse, stopped in front of Ray. Sheriff Dolan started, "you were right Coop. Those animals were waiting for us beyond the Lewis gulley and after the last bend, started shooting at us from boulders, as we were stuck in the open like sitting ducks. I am devastated to admit that I lost four good friends, two with serious gunshots, and the others who are acting like they saw the gates of hell. Be careful and remember to even the odds since you're going against deadly killers without a backup."

Ray continued but more cautiously. When he arrived at the Lewis gulley, he decided to get off the trail and try to get a view of the waiting outlaws. It was slow going amongst the trees, but suddenly he had a clear 200-yard view of the outlaws. Stepping down he pulled out of his rolled- up bedroll a long-range rifle, the telescoped Winchester 1876 in a 45-70 caliber. Setting on an old stump he spotted an idiot sitting on top of his protective boulder. Ray knew he could hit a coffee cup at 200 yards when using the 8X telescope. After taking aim on center mass, he squeezed the trigger and the outlaw was violently knocked back like a cotton doll hit by a hard ball. The result was total mayhem.

The outlaws were running about, as the leader yelled, "he is shooting at us with a long-range gun and we are like ducks on a carnival shelf. Get to your horses and we are out of here." One acolyte said, "but boss, Shorty had his $5,000 in his pants pocket!" "Who cares, go ahead and get it so the lawman can shoot your dumb head off. The rest of us, let's go and we'll meet at our hideout." The hesitant made a quick decision to save his hide as he followed his buddies at a full gallop.

With the outlaws rushing about, Ray was never able to get a second shot off. Walking into the outlaws' ambush site, he found the $5,000, and confirmed the outlaw's name with a letter addressed to him as well as seeing a burnished, C P Bummer, on the back of the outlaw's holster. Trailing the outlaw's horse, he resumed his tracking along the trail.

*

Following Ray from afar, they were certain to not make a visible dust cloud. Elle would periodically stop and spot him thru her telescopic lens. When he stopped for the night, she waited till dark and then slowly walked down the road. After tying her horse in some grass with a rivulet, she moved in close but stayed protected by the tree line. Ray had started a fire to cook beans and coffee. With the fire down to coals, he made a false stuffed bedroll near the fire, and hid behind his saddle some 25 feet away.

Come daybreak, Ray got up, went to the bushes to relieve his bladder, and do his daily business. Elle kept him in his telescope and got an eyeful. After he returned to the camp site, Browny's ears perked up and he started to growl. Elle could not see what he was growling at and decided to let Browny go fetch the likely rabbit—as she was planning to relieve her full bladder. With her britches down, Browny made contact and the result was not a screeching rabbit, but a wild man screaming for his buddies to shoot the wolf.

Ray pulled his Peacemaker out but could not see where the presumed assassin was located. At the sound of the screaming man, Elle pulled up her trousers and saw a sight she would never forget. High in a pine tree was a man pointing a rifle at Ray. In that instant, Elle recognized for the first time in her life that it was time to kill, or Ray would be killed. By instinct, she released the shotgun's tang safety, placed her finger on the double barrel shotgun's rear trigger, which controlled the long-range barrel, and squeezed it. The blast pushed a heavy smoke cloud all over Ray's head as he collapsed to the ground. The blast had a drastic effect as the tree shooter lost his rifle and his footing. As he came tumbling down, the branches were destroying his face and head as he finally hit the ground headfirst. Ray turned around and saw Elle for the first time.

There was no time for words as hoof beats were heard along the trail to the campsite. Three outlaws were bearing down on Ray. Two were firing their handguns at Ray as one was firing at Elle. Being on horseback did not help their aim as Ray put two down with a double tap of his Peacemaker. Elle had felt a hot sting on her left hip but managed to fire the short-range open barrel and blew the outlaw right out of the saddle.

The first words out of Elle's mouth were, "like you said, some of us are not meant to die young. But, that don't mean we can't catch a bullet." Ray responded quickly, and after unbuttoning her fly, he yanked her trousers down to the knees, then followed by yanking down the bloody underpants. Elle was stunned as she said, "maybe it would be nice to maintain some degree of modesty?" "No time for that, let's stop the bleeding. After a careful exam, he admitted that it was a superficial cut that had bled a lot. Ray then added, "I will need to place a few stitches so lay down so you don't pass out when you see the needle."

Elle reacted by squatting down. "What are you doing, I can't put stitches with you in that position?" "I AM PEEING." I had to pee before the shooting started. There, now put those stitches in and let's be done with it." "While standing?" "Yes, I'm a big girl. Just remember the damage is on top of my hip not in my crotch, so don't peek at my private parts, heh?" "Why not, you already gazed at my manly member thru a telescopic lens when I did my morning business." "Yes, that is true, you are hung like a horse—likely two hands. Touché, we are even, so let's start the stitches!" "But you still owe me, for I didn't use a telescope to enlarge the parts like you did, heh?" With that serene and threatening look, Ray applied carbolic acid to start the procedure. With clean sterile dressings in place, Ray removed her destroyed and bloody underpants and pulled up her trousers.

*

After gathering the outlaw firearms, and collecting the pocket cash of $30,189, the Duo loaded the dead outlaws onto their horse saddles, and secured them in place. They then sat down to make breakfast, have a talk, get acquainted, and all before returning to town.

Ray started, "why on earth did you do this?" "Because I am tired of being poor, have no purpose in life, live alone, and have no future!" "But how does going thru a shootout, that could have killed you, make those issues go away?" "By proving to you that Browny and I can be your backup, that I can shoot and both of us can kill when necessary." "To what goal?" "I want to become your bounty hunting partner!"

Ray paused and said, "that means we travel together, live together, and often require to use the same hotel room or a shared bedroll on a cold night—and not always providing privacy when bathing or performing natures demands." "So what, we already shared peeking at our privates but it didn't start a wild copulation. Hey, we are adults, and if consenting adults choose to have something happen, then it is no one's business." "But you will be shunned by the holier-than-thou, the do-gooders, and the prim-and-proper." "What is different than a single gal living alone with a dog. There is already talk that Browny is servicing me"—as Browny was covering his face with his front paws.

"Well Elle Belton, with a double L and two E's, there is no doubt you have sand, can shoot, appears trustworthy, somewhat pleasing to any man's eye, and with a great dog. So, you have a deal on a trial basis." Elle jumped up and gave Ray a kiss on his cheek with a very personal hug. "So let's have some breakfast of bacon, beans, biscuits, and coffee."

With the utensils packed, the Duo was ready to mount when Ray started counting money. When asked what he was doing, he said, "the finders' fee for returning $35,000 is 10% or $3,500. Here is your half, or $1,750, and you are no longer poor." Elle looked shocked, took the pile of cash, then put it in Ray's hand. "We are partners, so put it in the bank under our joint partnership. Instead, I would like half of the $189 so I can buy vittles for my house since I will be having a guest tonight and for nights to come!" "And who might that be?" As she sat in the saddle, she added, "play your cards right and you might become a long-term boarder, heh?"

*

The trip back to town was a quiet one until they stopped for the first break at a full stream to water the horses. It was Elle who broke the silence by asking, "this is all new to me, so where do we establish some permanent headquarters?" "I've been working in Texas for several years and I always seem to come back to New Braunfels!" "Really, well other than the fact that this is where I've lived all my life, have a house within a mile of town, and I really like living here; but why are you favoring this town?"

Ray paused but quickly said, "for a multitude of reasons. The town is ideally located on a busy strip between San Antonio and Waco. This is a quiet location with a population of 2,000 people whereas in 1880 there were 8,000 people in Waco and Austin, plus a whopping 18,000 in San Antonio. With the railroad running regularly between Waco and San Antonio, there is access to any towns on this strip, especially San Marcos and Killeen, and all within the same day. Plus, Sheriff Dolan is fair dealing with me as a bounty hunter—which is not always the case in other towns." "So, you are thinking we might get some business from all the other towns and cities along this +- 180-mile-long strip?" "Yes. Keep in mind, with the telegraph, any criminal activity along this strip will be reported to all the lawmen between Waco and San Antonio."

Elle paused, "how would that benefit us?" "We would give Sheriff Dolan a fee for every referral to assist other lawmen—all above board and perfectly legal." "Wow, that sounds like a plan."

Their next stop was for lunch. After the horses were attended to and brought to grass, the Duo prepared coffee and a cold roast beef sandwich. Sitting in the shade, Ray broached the subject of housing. "So you mentioned that you have a house within a mile of town. Any idea where I could find a boarding house that offers laundry and three meals a day?" "There is no need for that. I say you move in with me and we'll bring our laundry to Mister Lu and go to a diner several times a week while we batch our other meals together. We'll pay for our needs out of the partnership account. What do you say, shall we try it?"

"I'm willing to try it, but again, as we discussed, what will people think of a single man living with a single woman?" "Oh heck, 90% of people will say that they wished it could be them—and to heck with that snobbish 10%. After a few capers to save community merchants or people, we'll have 100% support, heh?" "Ok, well let's get going if we want to drop these bodies to the sheriff, buy some vittles, start a joint bank account, and maybe buy a buggy/harnessed horse for local traveling." "Sure, why not, I have a 20-acre fenced in pasture and a stable for four horses—but maybe arrange for a hay, straw, and an oats delivery."

*

As was common, arriving in town with a caravan of a half dozen bodies strapped to saddles, it attracted a crowd. When they arrived at the sheriff's office, Sheriff Dolan came outside carrying an envelope. "Well Coop, what have you got this time?" "I was after the Hollister gang when they attacked me with every intention of terminating my life. The sheriff walked around and said, "this one is missing a throat and windpipe, this one looks like he fell from a tree, these two were shot in the front chest and this one got peppered in the chest with buckshot. Where is the sixth one?" "Eaten by buzzards and coyotes, here is his name on his holster and a letterhead—C P Bummer. Plus the bank's $35,000—minus 10%."

Still holding that envelope, Sheriff Dolan said, "here are the bounty vouchers for the Simpson gang plus the sale of horses, tact, and guns. It comes to a total of $4,691." Ray opens the envelope and hands the sheriff $291 and adds, "that is for doing the legwork to accumulate the funds." "Very good, I'll see what I can find out what bounty is on their heads and will get back to you. I assume you want to sell the guns and horses, heh?" "For sure!"

The Duo then went to the bank and deposited the Simpson vouchers into the newly created joint account. Realizing what Ray had just done, she asked him to step aside so they could talk. "Why did you put that money in our joint account. It seems to me that the account should have its first deposit with the Hollister account." "Go along with this for now and I will explain things later."

The cashier then made both sign the joint account and they then each got bank books. To shock Elle even more, Ray arranged to do a wire transfer from Amarillo and Houston Wells Fargo banks to this new joint account. Once out of the bank, Elle asked for an explanation. "I don't feel right in inheriting your life's work." "Elle, I have no living relatives and no heirs that I know of. If something happens to me, or even you, then with both our names on the account, you don't need a will or a probate court order to continue your life, and you will not be left in a lurch!" "Well Ok, since it is done, let's let it slide for now, heh?"

"Great, now let's go buy a buggy and a harnessed horse. Then we'll fill the back with vittles to restock your house." "Yes, with only coffee on the shelf and eggs in the chicken coop, we actually need to restock the larder from A to Z."

The livery was owned by Enos Rutledge. He sold the Duo a nice one-seater buggy, with a trunk type unit in the rear, and a four-year-old well trained harnessed gelding for $200, including the harness. They then stopped at Halligan's Feed Store and arranged for a delivery of first crop hay, straw, and oats. Next was Kingston Energy to order firewood and coal. Their last stop was Zeke Holiday's General Store. After making introductions*, they went thru Elle's grocery list. Mona Holiday then took Elle in the back as they came out with a bag of personals to be added to the pile. The total bill came to $79 and Ray opened a credit account in both their names with the $79 payment and a $100 deposit.

Moseying to Elle's house in their new buggy, with both horses and Browny trailing the buggy, she was wool gathering and started laughing. Ray asked what was so funny. "It is a strange feeling as if we just got back from our honeymoon and are setting up house, heh?" "No, marriage would be much simpler than becoming business partners and living together—but we will manage, heh?"

*

Arriving at the house, they unloaded the vittles on the porch and drove the buggy into the carriage lean-to. Afterwards, the three horses were brought in the stable for a feeding and watering. Walking back to the house they stopped in the chicken coop and picked up a dozen eggs since the neighbor had not yet done his daily visit. They then brought the groceries in the house and set them on the kitchen table. That is when Elle gave Ray a grand tour.

"As you can see, this is a one room house with the dining table being the center of the room. Standing here, the furthest left-hand wall includes a hand pump well, the kitchen sink and a large work countertop. On the back-wall is the kitchen stove with oven and a hot water tank. Over the sink and stove are cabinets for eating utensils and dry goods. The back-wall is finished with a hutch and more cabinets. The right-side wall is for storage. First are these wide doors that hold back a Murphy bed and my old thick mattress. Then we have a utility closet, a walk-in clothing closet with shelves and a pipe bar for long clothing, then a chamber pot closet for middle of the night use, and then a door to the outside wooden sidewalk to the privy. Also note that once on the wooden sidewalk, there is a back door to the chamber pot closet to facilitate the emptying of the pot. Last is a business desk." "So far so good!"

The front wall has the 4-foot-wide field stone fireplace with the sofa and two lounge chairs facing the firebox. Then a firewood rack followed by the front door and the coat closet. Last of all the wall to the kitchen sink is for guns and reloading. The table is full of reloading presses and paraphernalia with overhead cabinets for loading components, and then a large gun and gear closet." "Everything seems well located. I only have questions about this reloading hobby you seem to have, but that will be for another day. For now, let's place the vittles in the cabinets or in your cold spot. Then, I couldn't help but notice you have your own shooting range with a natural berm. I would like to see what you can do with speed shotgun reloading during a gunfight, and how well you can handle that DA revolver with a funny looking grip."

Walking to the range, Ray set up some tin cans. For the shotgun test he set up four, quart size cans. "From cowboy port arms, on my call, load two shells and fire at will, then unload the spent shells and repeat on the last two cans." With a stopwatch in hand, Ray yelled fire. To his amazement, and in a fast but fluid motion, the shotgun opened, Elle spindly fingers pulled two shells from a special two shell holster, and dropped them in the barrels—more like threw them in the empty barrels from a distance of several inches. Boom/boom.

Elle quickly released the barrels and as the shotgun opened the spent shells were mechanically ejected over her right shoulder, loaded two more shells, closed the barrels, and fired twice more. Ray kept looking at his stopwatch and finally said, "you did that is 8 seconds. I saw it and still don't believe my own eyes. Miss Elle, that is not a born natural talent, that is acquired after hundreds and even thousands of attempts, heh?" "Yes, many times over the past months while in training."

"Training, heh? We'll talk about that later, now let's see what you can do with that odd-looking revolver." "This odd thing is a DA revolver in 41 Long Colt, (called Colt 1877 Thunderer), and the grip is different to enable anyone to pull the long trigger since the shooter does not need to pull back the hammer for the gun to fire—like you need to do with your Peacemaker!" "True, but my Peacemaker has been altered so I can fan one shot after another by keeping my finger on the pulled back trigger, while fanning the hammer with my left hand." "Well, I think I can match your speed. Let's set up 12 cans and see who finishes shooting first, assuming all six cans were hit."

On a signal, the two shootists started dueling. It was a sequence that consisted of one discharge after another, sometimes two shots together. With one can left standing, the shooters heard, Ba/Bang. The shooters looked at each other and neither knew who shot last. With smoke everywhere, Ray said, "I think the coffee is ready and I can't wait to hear the story how a young good-looking gal could have spent the time to become such a top notch shootist."

Back at the cabin, Elle invited Ray to clean his firearm as she did the same to hers. Being they had fired black powder, the guns would corrode and ruin the rifling and its accuracy if left uncleaned. It was Elle who took the opportunity to explain how her double barrel shotgun had been altered to have the barrel release in front of the trigger guard instead of ahead of the tang safety, and include extractors, ejectors, and self cocking upon closing the barrels. Ray was impressed at the gunmanship and promised to visit Sonny's gun-shop at the first opportunity.

Sitting with fresh coffee, Ray got right to the subject on his mind. "Well Miss Elle, E-double l-E, please start from the early years in school to the present. I know that any proficient shootist has to have had an interesting past, heh?" "Well, I don't know how interesting it will be, but I assure you my past had all to do with my currently chosen profession."

***

CHAPTER 2

Getting to know Elle

"I don't remember much of the elementary school years except for the 7th and 8th grades. Other than scholastics, I became the known defender for the mild, meek, and susceptible kids who were targets for developing bullies. Many days, I got into an all-out fight with coward bullies. After a solid punch to their nose, they would run to the teacher complaining how I had attacked them. Of course, mom would pick me up at school and knew by my clothing that I had put down another bully, and with an impish smile, would say nothing."

"Anyways my true recollection started when I went to high school. The cute girls saw me as an underdeveloped tomboy who did not fit amongst the elite—mostly blonde girls. Early on my dad recognized my social lot and decided that I should know how to defend myself, so on my 14th birthday, he gave me a New Line Colt SA 22 revolver in 22 short or long before the days of the long rifle cartridge. His directions were clear, 'learn to point & shoot on the cheap 22 bullets, and then I'll give you a real revolver and show you how to fast draw, speed shoot, and hit your target.'"

"For a year I shot every day in our own range and on my 15th birthday he handed me a Colt 1877 DA in 38 short/long (Colt Lightning)—plus a reloading center to reload my 38 cases. I enjoyed reloading and shooting, as well as sharing the time with my high school girlfriend. My dad worked in a machine shop that made hardened carbon steel parts for Colt firearms. So he beefed up my revolver, did an action job, and made it a smooth operating machine."

"Year after year I enjoyed reloading and shooting for pleasure after I had learned the basics in fast draw. Dad enjoyed following my progress as mom started to wonder how such a hobby could ever help her daughter find a man and earn a living. Her fears were well founded as I graduated from high school with no plans for the future. Most of the school gals were engaged to be married but I just seemed lost. I spent the summer floundering but promised my parents that I would have some direction come September. Yet, a catastrophic event occurred in late August that put me on a specific path."

"Whoa, before we move on, weren't there any men in your life?" "Now stop to think. I didn't experience a precocious puberty like blonde gals, and when I did start puberty as a Junior, I also had a growth spurt. By my senior year I hit 6 feet tall and had a full bosom and bum. None of the guys were tall and standing next to them we looked like a 'mutt and jeff' duo. Even during my floundering summer, eligible men only wanted to get free rein to my love nest—but that's another subject for another time." "Sorry to interrupt, please go back to the event at the end of August."

"It was a Saturday night when mom and dad had gone dancing. They were expected back by midnight when they were late getting home. Suddenly there was a knock at the door and our wolfdog just about ate the door. When the visitor identified himself, things changed. Sheriff Dolan stood in the doorway, holding his hat, and crying so hard he could not speak clearly." There was a long pause as Ray kept quiet. "My parents had been waylaid by highwaymen and had been both shot to death."

*

After the funeral, I went into a profound depression. It was Doc Summers who helped me out of the melancholy when he said, 'there is no one on this earth that can save you. You must save yourself. Find a goal and go for a life-saving event, for the way you are going now, only death awaits you!'"

"Well I turned a hobby into a profession. I had inherited the paid-up house, land, $500 bank account, plus my dad's $1,000 life insurance policy at work. For months I practiced shooting the newly acquired double barrel shotgun and the beefed-up Colt Lightning. When I was ready, I found my dad's beefed-up Colt Thunderer and exchanged it for my less powerful Colt Lightning."

"On that infamous evening, I left home at midnight in a rented horse and buggy. As expected, I was detained by two masked highwaymen. Their line was a cliché; 'your money or your life.' As prepared, I handed them a leather pouch and added, 'all I have are gold nuggets.' Those idiots were so fixated in opening the leather pouch, that when they pulled out some barnyard stones, my 41 long colt Thunderer barked twice and both highwaymen were blown out of their saddles."

Again Ray waited patiently. "I walked to the first man with a sucking chest wound and asked him if he was the one who shot my parents. When he spit at me, I shot him in the mouth. I then asked the other, with a nonfatal chest wound, and he quickly admitted that they were the shooters. This one said, "Shorty stupidly grabbed the lady's breast as she pulled off his mask and immediately admitted that she knew him. The man knew the die was cast as he went for his gun. We had no choice but to shoot them both to protect our identity." "I then said, 'so you killed two beautiful people for pocket change—what kind of animal predator are you. We kill coyotes, and we hang psychopaths, but I don't have time to hang you, so go see Shorty in hell'—as I shot him in the heart."

Ray moved his hand across the table and held her hand in total quietude. It was some time before Elle's tears dried up. Eventually he said, "so now you are on an altruistic campaign to rid the world of this kind of trash, heh?" "Well I don't know if that is what I've become, some days it sounds like revenge and or restitution" "No, I suspect you have become a Paladin—one who has a mission to rid the world of predators that ravage the innocent. From experience, trust me, it takes a lot of 'panache' to stay on this dangerous crusade, heh?"

*

"So after the prosecutor called the shooting a case of robbery at gunpoint, and self-defense on my part, I started looking for a way to continue my crusade. That was months later when you arrived with the Simpson gang and said you were going after the Hollister gang, by yourself. I knew then that you had become my ticket to the future."

"Well there is no doubt, you pushed the envelope, but with so much sand and beauty, what chance would any man have to say no, heh? Anyways, I guess it is my turn to tell you my story. My high school years were my formative years. As a freshman, I worked in a gun-shop nights and weekends. In no time I was doing action jobs and then became the man to repair broken firearms. It was natural for me to see how the gun mechanism was working and what part had gone bad to cripple the firearm. Along with that, I spent many hours practicing fast-draw and gun fanning. That is when we started using hardened steel parts to neutralize the strain on guns during fanning."

"By graduation, I knew I was heading for my own gun-shop when the brake was put on by Enos Straus. For the next two years I trained and learned the bounty hunting trade till recently when Enos got a heart condition and had to retire. In truth, after this last caper with the Hollister gang, I was planning to retire and use my bank account to buy a Main Street storefront and start my own gun-shop to specialize in broken firearms. With both of my parents gone from a lethal fever illness, I had no family left and had no reason to return to Colorado and suffer during the cold winter months. So for the reasons I gave you earlier, New Braunfels, was as good a place to settle down as anywhere else, heh?"

Elle was thinking and finally asked, "did I push the issue and forced you to continue living by the gun?" "No, I am a fatalist, I will only say that meeting you changed my path. At this time, I am not sure why I changed my mind, but am willing to see where my decision takes us."

*

Elle hesitated but eventually said, "I have so many questions about our association, could we do a 'question and answer' session to clear the air?" "Absolutely, fire away!"

1. "What kind of capers will we be willing to take on?" "Despite what you expect, it will not be bounty hunting for high bounties. We'll take a new approach, we will be supporting our lawmen—and in town we will support Sheriff Dolan as well as any lawmen between Waco and San Antonio. We will work as a result of lawmen asking for our help. Stop to think of what crimes the local sheriffs are exposed to and tell me they can take care of these without help. I am

referring to killer gangs, negotiate kidnappings, protect abused wives, catching rapists, rustling, range wars, bank robberies, infidelity issues, and human trafficking just to name a few. So the help I am referring to is you, me, and Browny along with the sheriff and a deputy."

2. "Any chance of adding more members to our team?" "Absolutely, it is a matter of choosing the right one. We may need a tracker, another shootist, a snoopy investigator, or specialists in case we start specializing. We may even need a second team if we start spreading out of town. That is too far ahead to be more specific."

3. "It still sounds like we would be 'guns for hire.'" "Not necessarily, I look at us as 'Culminators.' We will make things happen, we will bring an issue to a head, reach a resolution, even if it involves gun play."

4. "Why do I get the impression that there are many outlaws on this strip between Waco and San Antonio?" "There are. Stop to think if you were an outlaw, would you stay in the cold and snow country of Colorado or Montana to spend your loot, compared to southwest Texas where it is warm, dry, and plenty of saloons and

whorehouses. Plus it is within 150 miles from San Antonio to Del Rio where they can cross into Mexico if the law is after them in Texas. Now New Braunfels has an American/German culture whereas San Antonio is more Spanish based with an American/Mexican background."

5. "Unlike bounty hunting where bounties are well known, how do we generate income being a lawman's helper—for there has to be renumeration when placing our lives on the line?" "It is true that stopping a wife beater has more satisfaction than income, but fear not, there will be plenty of wanted career criminals with a price on their heads."

6. "Can you give me some tips on how to handle capers?" "Every caper is different and I have two years' experience but I'm still learning. There are some facts and methods that are true no matter what the capers are. Here are some examples that I will elaborate on when the situation arises: any nighttime camp is made into a safe camp, how to convince a resistant outlaw to give us info we need, how to use methods to equilibrate the balance of firepower, and how to use a dog—to be specific as nighttime security. to track outlaws

and victims by their sense of smell, avoid danger by 'dog sense,' and use them on the attack as an extra shooter. Also don't give outlaws special privileges for they will kill you any chance they get. A hanging offense quadruples an outlaw's aggressiveness since he knows he will hang if arrested. And last of all, never turn your back on an outlaw—even the ones that seemingly surrendered peacefully."

7. "The idea of using 'jungle warfare' to disable a gang is intriguing. Can you give me an idea how that works." "There are two methods I use. The first is 'hit and run.' An example is to set up a loaded shotgun on a tripwire over the trail. When activated by man or horse, both barrels fire and usually take an outlaw out of the fight. The second method is to 'booby trap' a campsite with wolf and bear traps on the foot path to the bushes, or throw an angry hornets' nest onto sleeping drunk outlaws. You'll see more tricks that I have developed over the years as I choose the items to match each situation—but dynamite is by far the best tool."

8. "I was surprised when you mentioned ways to use Browny. To me a growling wolfdog pulling at

an outlaw's crotch would make him speak with diarrhea of the mouth. Can you think of other uses for him?? "Yes, keep those bums' hands off your body." After some laughter, Ray added, "you do realize that winning a gunfight depends on who has an edge. Well to gussy you up with revealing upper and lower cleavage will give us a definite edge since an outlaw's brain is either on his handgun hand or on his loins, heh? You cannot doubt that you are pleasing to the eye for you are no booglin!" "Which is?" "Short, fat, and ugly!"

9. "You mentioned that each situation is unique. So how do you adjust your approach?" "A planning meeting. Agreeing to an organized set up will be in our favor. Let's take a gang arrest in a saloon for example:

- How many outlaws are there and are they all in the saloon.
- Any missing outlaw may show up unexpectedly. So windows or doors have to be covered.
- Know the location of all the outlaws in the saloon.

- Use Browny to locate outlaws with guns under the tables.
- Equilibrate gun power. A sheriff with a double barrel is good for two outlaws, you are good for four with your tricked coach shotgun, Browny is good for one, and I am good for 3 or 4 if there are no gunfighter fast draw shootists in the group.
- Is the gang all liquored up or alert.
- Are there any locals or deputies who are good with a gun and capable of helping out if we are short of fire power. If not and we are outnumbered, then it is better to avoid the battle and be able to fight another day, heh?"

10. "Last for now, there will be plenty of off days between capers, how do we occupy our time?" "Like any profession, the day will come when we'll not be able to continue this dangerous lifestyle. Until then, we need to keep our gun skills up to snuff and at the same time start working on our next career." "Oh really, like what?" "I have a few possibilities in mind but I assure you, when we see it, we'll know it is for us."

*

Elle said, "well, I don't know about you but I am getting hungry. Let's go turn the horses out to pasture, bring in the chickens, get some potatoes, carrots, and onions out of the garden; and we'll boil potatoes and carrots, fry the onions, and pan cook the two steaks we bought today. For dessert, we have store bought sugar cookies with fresh coffee." "Sounds like a plan. But don't forget, we have to clean your wound and change the dressing." "I just knew you weren't going to forget that!" "Oh heck, it is nothing and I promise not to peek, heh?" "Yeah right, when my trousers drop your eyes fixate on my lower triangle." "Well, brown is a nice color, heh?"

After washing and sterilizing the wound, he had Elle bend over so he could get the dressing tape properly applied After the ordeal Elle said, "I finally know why you supposedly need to have me bend over, It is not to ease taping the dressing, it is because you get to see my 'flower.' Am I not right?" "Oh Elle, that is not my normal nature to do such a thing." "But you are not denying it?" "Well let me say, did you know you are a virgin?" The coffee mug went flying and Ray thought it best to go check on the horses.

While preparing supper, Ray apologized for his behavior. He was more than forgiven when he said, "a man should never joke about a woman's choice of remaining chaste till she met the right man." Nothing more was said till the Duo sat down to eat their first home cooked meal together.

Ray had been away from people for so long that he had to adjust to someone talking so freely from one subject to another, even while eating. To Ray, it seemed that Elle was behaving as if they were long lost friends, but in a way, Ray was happy with that. After several sugar cookies with coffee Elle suggested, "what do you say you start a fire in the fireplace as I start cleaning the dishes?" "Deal, then I'll wipe them dry and learn to place them in the appropriate cabinets."

While wiping the dishes, he asked, "so what do you like to do in the evenings once sitting by the fire?" "I like to read." "What, dime novels?" "No, in the cabinet above my loading center is my library on guns, reloading, current new models, and much info on this new smokeless powder coming soon." "Really!" "Yes, but tonight we should read the two local newspapers to find out what is going on in town for sales and entertainment. Plus we can talk about which merchants to deal with that are not always ready to skin you alive."

Sitting in each of their lounging chairs, Ray said, "there are way too many advertisements. So how do you choose which place to do business with?" "Easy, I've lived here all my life and it is not so easy for someone new in town. So here is my go-to-list. We've already dealt with President Willis at the bank, Zeke and Mona Holiday's store, Enos Rutledge livery, Doc Summers, Halligan's Feed and Seed store, and of course my favorite Sonny's gun-shop. Now here is a list of less frequented establishments: Kingston's Coal and Firewood, Harrison Garments, Labor's Apothecary, Winnie's or Dixie's Diners, Madison Hotel and Fine Dining, the Rusty Bucket Saloon, Myrtle's Haberdashery, Sam's Tonsorial Shop, Mackenzie's Leather, Blackie Washburn—The Smithy, Telegraph office c/o Waldo Sonar, Saint Andrew, Methodist Church c/o Pastor Genson, RR freight and passenger terminal c/o Stan Emerson, and of course the post office c/o Snake Eyes MacDonald."

"Goodness, this is only a town of 2,000 people and the list of places we can spend money is endless and sounds like a big city." "Speaking of that, remember when you quoted population numbers along this strip in 1880?" "Yes." Well, look at page four. The population of Austin, San Antonio, and Waco have doubled today in 1990. Austin and Waco are both at 15,000 and San Antonio at 35,000. But New Braunfels has not changed at 2,000." "Good for us, it will grow fast enough; so let's not wish expansion till the Cowboy Era comes to an end."

"Cowboy Era, now that is an interesting subject. So when did it begin and when is it expected to end?" "Well, the beginning will always be contested but most agree it started after the Civil War when the cattle drives started, the Westward Migration was continuing, then the Buffalo were harvested, followed by the railroad across the west, as young men went west and ranching life became king. Along with all this, were the notorious outlaws all over the west. Soon the Industrial Revolution is expected to change society." "So how many years do we have left before we have to change our ways along with the Industrial Revolution?" "Fifteen, max of twenty years." "Perfect, a full generation which will include the best years of our lives, heh?"

*

The Duo was reading the newspaper when a horse was heard coming in the driveway. Ray got up to see who was coming, as he suddenly grabbed Elle and sat next to her on the sofa. "I suspect I know why Sheriff Dolan would make a visit tonight, since we just left him today. Anyways, trust me and play along so we can buffalo him. When he leaves, I will explain. When the sheriff knocked, Browny came alive but was turned down by Elle's command. "Come in sheriff." As he entered, Ray put his arm over Elle's shoulder and brought her in. "Well sheriff, this must be a social call, since you haven't had time to get vouchers on the Hollister gang." "Oh darn it all, this is the part of the job I hate the most!"

"Stop right there and let me make it easy for you. I have found a wonderful woman and I'm not letting her go just to satisfy the nosy snobs who were never fortunate to find a mate." Elle, somewhat surprised, looked at Ray and then the sheriff. "Is that true, Sheriff?" "Well yes and no. There are some that are jealous, some that consider cohabitating unmarried couples a sin, and some just need to be reassured that you are here with a man at your own free will. If that is the case, then I congratulate you both for having found a mate and I will take care of those in town who cannot let well enough alone." Elle said nothing and planted a lingering kiss on Ray's cheek. "I assure you sheriff that you are looking at a very contented single female, and I am not about to let this man escape," "That's all I wanted to hear, and again I am happy for you. Plus, the Missus and I will soon have you over for supper, for my wife is eager to meet the man who captured the most eligible female in our town."

As the sheriff was on his horse, Ray whispered that they should provide the "coup de gras." With an unknowing nod, Ray put his hands around her back and planted the most passionate kiss on the unsuspecting Elle. When the front door closed, they separated and Elle said, "the sheriff is gone, so you can stop pretending." "Do you think I was pretending, because I didn't get that impression with your lingering response." "Yes, well it appears we both may have gotten caught up in the moment, heh?" After some minutes, the Duo sat next to each other on the sofa and resumed reading the newspaper. It seemed that there was tension in the air when Elle asked, "what would you like to do tomorrow?" "You may think this is ridiculous, but I would like to learn how to reload brass ammo and shotgun shells." "Well I'll be snookered, I would enjoy teaching you the art of reloading. We should have a pleasant day. For now, it has been a busy and revealing day, so I suggest we get ready for bed and get some well-deserved sleep."

*

Elle opened the doors to the Murphy bed and pulled out the double mattress. "I strongly suggest we sleep on this mattress next to the kitchen stove." "Why, what's wrong with the Murphy bed?" "It has a steel bar across your mid back and you'll wake up lame. The mattress is a new 10-inch one with springs and you'll enjoy the comfort it provides." "But, that means we will be sleeping together." "I am sure you will act like a gentleman, besides we are business partners and according to the sheriff we are an item, heh?" "That was to satisfy the busy-bodies and you know that!" "Whatever!"

After banking the kitchen stove with two shovelfuls of coal, she mentioned that "if either of us get up to use the chamber pot, then bank the fire with two more shovelfuls of coal to keep the house temperature up. Afterwards, under the kerosene lamp, Ray dressed down to his union suit, as Elle started stripping down, with her back to Ray, and jumped out of her clothes to expose her new bra and panties. "Where did you get those?" "Mona Holiday gave me her new samples from Miss Vicky's apparel. Do you like them?" "Really, well of course, they are really sexy, especially on the right body, but they don't cover all your female parts, heh?" With an impish smile, she stripped, again with her back to Ray, and redressed in her favorite two-piece flannel baggy pajama, and jumped under the sheets as she turned the lamp off.

Minutes passed with both bedmates laying on their backs with ample free space between them. Out of nowhere, Ray said, "what was done is done. You cannot turn back the clock. Besides, at times, one has to express one's feelings. I have no regret." Time paused again, when Elle suddenly did an about face turn, and half straddled Ray. Without hesitation, she planted a full mouth kiss on a surprised Ray. "Is there any doubt how I feel about you—and this is real to me even if we've only known each other for one full day. Now spoon me, I am cold. Elle brought her back to Ray's front, and the two spent the night snuggled together with Ray's arm over her waist.

*

At 3AM, Elle woke up and had to use the chamber pot. Getting up, she lit the kerosene lamp to get to the chamber closet and then went to bank the kitchen stove with more coal. Getting back in bed she couldn't help but notice that Ray's union suit was unbuttoned and his massive male tool was sticking out in full tumescence. With another impish smile, she turned the lamp off and resumed her spooning position, but this time, using some creative positioning to account for a full bone poking at her.

Ray woke at daybreak and got up. With free time, he visited the privy for private needs, emptied the chamber pot, brushed his teeth, and even shaved. When all his ablutions were taken care of, he started preparing breakfast. With coffee boiling, he cut up left over potatoes to make home-fries, sliced bacon and bread for toast, and prepared a half dozen eggs for frying. When the coffee was ready, he brought a mug over and gently poked Elle awake. "Here is your coffee my queen. That's for feeding the fire last night." Elle sat up, thanked him, and went for the coffee. Three gulps later, she got up and ran to the privy.

Upon her return Ray said, "that was a heck of a bodily response to my coffee." "Yes, I usually bring my mug with me to the privy and take care of business. But it was nice of you to think of me." "Well, do your morning ablutions and I'll start the bacon and home-fries, and save the toast and eggs till you are done."

Once finished, she went ahead and set the table as she put the mattress away. Halfway thru breakfast she said, "I had forgotten how nice it was to wake up to coffee and an all-prepared breakfast. As partners, I'll make a deal with you. Since you are an early riser and I like to linger, if you make breakfast, we can each make our own cold lunch sandwich, and I will cook you a homemade supper each night." "Deal." "Plus I will help you to clean up the breakfast pans and utensils, if you do the same for supper." "Deal again. Now let's get going, for we are burning daylight and I have a lot to learn about reloading, heh?" "Piece of cake, I can teach you all you need to know in two hours, then it's practice, practice, and more practice!"

*

Elle had all the equipment set up for reloading brass centerfire ammo at one end of the bench and 12-gauge shotgun shells at the other end of the bench. The brass ammo required a single press for each of the four procedures: sizing and de-priming, priming, powder addition, bullet seating with crimping. Starting with the easy 38 Long Colt caliber, Elle had Ray do 100 rounds with the first press before moving to the second press. All the while, talking away with one fact after another. By lunch time, Ray had processed each of the 100 rounds thru the four presses and ended up with 100 rounds ready to shoot.

For lunch, the Duo made some cold rare roast beef sandwiches with fresh coffee. While eating, Ray said, "tonight I'll read your textbook on reloading brass, but for now, I am interested in how much of black powder we added and why use that cute mini brass cup to handle black powder?" "That cute brass cup held 21 grains of black powder by VOLUME and not by weight. That powder with a 150-grain lead bullet by WEIGHT yielded 777 fps and 201-foot-pounds of energy. The brass cup is to prevent a static electrical spark that would cause the black powder to explode, and that is also why you wore protective eyeglasses. Now to compare extremes, had we been loading 38 short, it would have been a smaller cup holding 18 grains of black powder by VOLUME, with a 100- grain bullet, and it would have been at +- 700 fps and +- 150 ft.-pounds- of energy. Now at the other end of the scale the 41 long colt with its 200- grain bullet, would also have had a larger cup to hold +- 23 grains of black powder by VOLUME, and at 750 fps would have more energy for knock down power at +- 240-ft.-pounds of energy." "Very good, that all makes sense to me!" "Now to make some sense in this energy knock down power, let's talk about 12-gauge OO Buckshot. Now 9 pellets are loaded with 70 grains of black powder at 1,300 fps.—or 12 pellets under 100 grains of black powder at the same velocity. Now each loaded round delivers an outstanding 1,500 ft. pounds of energy for 12 or 13 ounces of lead pellets—which is not comparable with the pistol caliber's energy. Of course the shotgun is reliable up to 40 yards whereas the pistol has the longer 75-yard range. There are many more facts about fps, ft.-pounds of energy, and knock down power in my books—more reading material for evenings, heh?"

That afternoon, Elle went over the steps in loading 12-gauge OO Buckshot using waxed paper hulls. With four presses she covered each step. Press # one was to de-prime the case and resize the brass base. The second was to prime and add the black powder by VOLUME. The third press was to add a thick waxed paperboard wad pressed onto the powder to separate the powder from the pellets. Then add manually nine or twelve 0.33-inch pellets as three per layer with a thin paperboard card on top of the last layer of pellets. The fourth press was a double one that starts the paper crimp and then finishes it over the paperboard card.

By 4PM, Ray had mastered both systems and was glad to stop for the day since he now knew that reading about reloading would make sense. Being early for supper, Ray suggested they do a dressing change. Once in the process he said, "this wound needs to soak in a soapy solution to clean up the dead tissues?" "Not a problem, there is a tub on wheels in the utility closet, bring it over and we'll use the hot water supply in the kitchen stove mixed with cold water for comfort."

With about 10 inches of warm water, Elle jumped in and started scrubbing. Ray took on the wound cleansing and when done, Elle said, "would you unsnap my bra and wash my back?" "Sure, but cover your chest to maintain some degree of modesty, heh?" "Well how ridiculous can that be, I just exposed my very private area during the dressing change and you need my breasts covered—really?" "Hey, I am just a man and I am already fully randy from just changing your dressings, so let's not push it since there is no more room in my trousers, heh? So please finish up yourself, get dried up, put on your new undies, and I will then apply a new dressing. Hopefully my distress will abate so I can sit down for a home cooked meal." With another of her impish smiles, Elle complied.

***

CHAPTER 3

The Gun-Shop

That evening, Ray started reading Elle's books on reloading. Throughout the evening, while both sitting on the sofa, Ray would ask questions and Elle would answer. After finishing the state-of-the-art text on the subject, Ray put the book down. As a spontaneous event, Ray put his hand on Elle's thigh. Elle responded as any willing participant would and snuggled up into Ray's arms. To his surprise, she said, "you do realize you have a horny virgin in your arms. Are you prepared to take on that responsibility; for I am not about to say no to you, now or ever!"

Ray paused and said, "I am prepared but not willing to take that step. I know how you feel about me and that is more important than any lustful intimacy at this juncture. Kiss me and reassure me that I am right." Well that was the request that opened the gate. The Duo kissed repeatedly and even let their hands roam. In due time, the heat of passion was getting close to explosion when Elle suggested that they stop before it would get to a point of no return.

To help decompress and dry up, the Duo went to the kitchen to warm up the coffee and have peanut-butter on soda crackers, as a bedtime snack. After hitting the mattress, the Duo went back into their spooning position, but this time, Elle took his hand from her waist and brought it to her bosom. During their goodnight kiss, he caressed both breasts as a sign of more advanced intimacy.

Morning came as the Duo found themselves at the breakfast table. Busy eating, they were both using that excuse to hold up on last night's course of events—or lack of events. Finally, Ray blurted it out, "will you explain why two consenting adults did not have a conjugal event last night?" Elle acted in the moment as if she already had the answer practiced. She said, "probably because we are falling in love and are both afraid to ruin it by lustful acts. If you are like me, as I think you are, I have been looking for a lifelong mate, and want to guarantee that I don't lose you on the way." "I am past the point of wandering away, you've got me hooked on a short line." As they were alerted by Browny of an incoming visitor, he stepped on the porch, but instead of barking and growling, his tail was wagging. Ray said, "guess we have an unexpected guest for breakfast." "Well, I'm glad you weren't changing my dressing, heh?"

Sheriff Dolan walked in and was not carrying a social facial expression. When he refused coffee, Ray said, "you are obviously preoccupied, so please, tell us what the problem is that has you in such a tizzy!" "There has been a gang holed up in the Rusty Bucket for the past two days. This morning I heard that our council president has been kept a hostage in the saloon until the town pays for his release to the tune of $5,000. These animals number eight and are part of the Humbolt gang that has been robbing homesteaders from Waco to here. They are all wanted dead or alive, but no one has been willing to go after them, since they arrived in Waco and moved along the strip when they finally arrived here a few days ago. This morning, they started torturing Amos, our councilman, since no one was offering a ransom payment. Every hour they do something awful to him since he screams out in pain for fifteen minutes. I need to put a stop to this, but me and my greenhorn deputy are not able to mount up a force against eight killer outlaws."

There was total silence as Elle asked, "so you are asking for our help?" "Yes, and we need to get more willing men involved." Ray looked at Elle and the sheriff as he said, "I can take three down myself." The sheriff added, "with a double barrel shotgun, I am good for two." As Elle added, "I am good for three with a reload, and we have Browny and Deputy Crandall as our backup if they have a surprise ninth member who is incognito." Ray then added, "let's gear up and get to releasing Amos before he loses more body parts, heh?"

*

The ride to town was somber. As soon as they arrived at the sheriff's office, the team heard a loud scream. Browny's ears perked up and was chomping to go but Elle ordered him to stay by her heel. After checking their guns, the sheriff took his shotgun out and loaded it. In no time the deputy was asked to stay outside the saloon and look for anyone pulling a gun and stop him at gun point.

Ray looked over the batwing doors and after careful recon stepped back and said, "Amos is on a table, nude from the waist down, and Humbolt himself if slamming his hog-leg grip at his toes to keep him dancing. Amos has most of his fingers dislocated backwards and is full of facial bruises. As far as where these animals are located, three are to the right of Amos and Humbolt and four are on his left. Elle said, "I'll take Humbolt and then the two on the front of the left table. Sheriff Dolan will take the two left over on the left table. And you Ray are responsible for the three on the right of Humbolt." Ray said, "that's a good plan, just make sure you have a solid target, don't have stray pellets hitting Amos, and let me do the talking. Just remember, when an outlaw goes for his gun, it is time to kill or be killed—don't wait for any outlaw's gun pointing at you."

On his signal, Ray entered first followed by Elle, Browny, and Sheriff Dolan. Ray yelled at Humbolt, "that's enough 'Bubba,' now holster your gun and let Amos down. On the count of three, Mad Dog Elle will blow your gun hand off, so be quick about it. "One, two"........"hold up, let's not be hasty, we were just having some fun. I'm putting my gun away,"

"Barkeep, have you got a couple of aprons to cover Amos?" "Sure do!" Now Humbolt, we know who you are. You've caused enough mayhem during your homesteader marauding. Plus you were holding a councilman for ransom. That is a hanging offense besides the fact that you are all wanted dead or alive. So Sheriff Dolan is arresting you. Now put your guns on the table and lift your hands up in surrender, or draw and make your play." "Why you pipsqueak, we'll crush you down like cockroaches you are. Humbolt went for his gun but with a neck shot,

Elle decapitated him. As his head landed on the table, it distracted his gang members as the firearms started blasting away. In ten seconds, no one could see anything in the saloon from the gun-smoke. When things cleared, Elle, Ray, and the sheriff were standing as Browny was watching the batwing doors and started growling. After a loud thump, a man appeared at the batwing doors with a gun in hand. Browny responded and took a bite out of the man's calf just above the boot's leather leggings. Elle saw the man point his gun down and was about to shoot Browny, as Elle quickly shot above the batwing doors. It was later that the undertaker had picked up the second body without a head on its shoulders. After the shootout, Ray paid spectators $2 each to help drag the outlaws onto the street as some were paid to clean up the bloody sawdust. At the end, the collected cash from the dead outlaws totaled $259 which was used to pay for damages and unpaid outlaw tabs.

Before leaving town, the sheriff had some points to make. "I will always be grateful for your help. Needless to say, I have earned my badge as far as Amos is concerned. Anyways, the bad part in all this is the notoriety you will get from this shootout with a gang of nine killers. Some lawmen will ask you for their help but ne'er do wells will end up challenging you to enhance their reputation. Well, despite this, I am still waiting on the Hollister vouchers as I will apply for the Humbolt vouchers after I sell the guns and horses, heh?" "For sure." "And by the way Elle, what do you load your Buckshot shells with these days; if this keeps up, they will call you the Guillotine Lady."

*

On the way home Elle said, "Guillotine Lady sounds better than Mad Dog Elle, don't you think?" "Either one is a moniker that will give us an edge since either name infers that you are UNHINGED." "I have to be unhinged to go into a gunfight before I ever had the chance to show you how much I love you." Ray took her hand and kissed it. "I feel the same way, and it's never too late to make a serious correction. Maybe tonight could be a good time to become committed lovers, heh?" Elle didn't have time to answer when Ray pulled on the reins and stopped the buggy in the middle of the street. Elle was lost as she said, "well not now, in the middle of the street!" "No dear, let's go to Dixie's for lunch and then next door to check out Sonny's gun-shop, heh? We have all night for private time, heh?" Elle was laughing so loud that she had to rush to Dixie's privy before having a wet accident.

The Duo sat down and had coffee to settle their nerves. Elle started by saying, "Ray you don't seem phased from the shootout. Why I am a pack of nerves and it is why I said what I did." "Stop right there, I may not show it after two years on the bounty hunting trail, but I am affected. It is never easy to kill a man and it wears heavy on me. But it is what I do and I try to cope the best I can. So trying to keep our mind off the job is a good thing to be good at. Now let's eat." The Duo ordered a platter of chicken salad sandwiches with unlimited coffee.

While eating, Elle had a brainstorm. "Is part of coping the reason we are going to Sonny's after lunch?" "Yes, I cannot lie. You are very astute. Looking at the display cases and the many shelved rifles and goods is relaxing plus we may see something we need or just plain want." "Well, you know that Sonny tricked out my Remington Hammerless Coach Shotgun and beefed up my 1877 DA in 41 Long Colt. Just keep in mind, Sonny is a genious gun designer and modifier as he does work for Colt, Remington, and likely other major gun manufacturers. On top of that he does action jobs, repairs firearms, and handles sales at the front customer desk. I know his wife Stella who also works several half days as the head salesperson. They live upstairs, raised two kids, and have been in business since before I was born. Plus they are the most pleasant couple that I know!" "That is an interesting historical background, so let's go in and see what the place looks like."

Walking in, Elle was stunned. "When did you make all these renovations?" Stella answered, "in the past month, now come here and give me a hug." Sonny came up and said, "so you are the famous 'Coop' who just put down the Hollister and Humbolt gangs?" "Yes sir, but I wasn't alone, I had Elle and her incredible shotgun as well as that reliable wolfdog." "Yes we heard. Anyways, what can we do for you?" "For now, we want to look around." "Go right ahead!"

The Duo was amazed at the layout. Elle pointed out that the repair and research shop was behind the front desk. Then a walk-in section with new rifles on the left wall and used ones on the right wall. After checking out the new ones, they moved on to a long glass display of handguns with a large storage room behind the glass display. The handguns ranged from SA and DA 22 revolvers to the modern DA Colt 1892 to the large 45 Long Colt Peacemaker, and many unknown models in-between. The shelves behind the glass display were loaded with ammo—but out of reach of customers. Pleased with the layout, the Duo decided to sit down next to the potbelly stove and munch on soda crackers. With the last customer out the door, the Duo started talking with the Greathouses. Elle started, "so why the rifle displays available to customers?" "Because it takes an extra employee to hand each rifle that they need to aim with. Now, they can take anyone in their hands and not bother us. Besides, they can't hide a rifle in their pockets like they could with handguns and ammo. That is why handguns are in the glassed display cases and ammo is out of reach."

Ray added, "this all makes sense plus I like the touch of a heating stove with free soda crackers. The only thing missing is free coffee. Stella added, "oh but we provide free coffee till 9AM as well as two pastries for a nickel." "Why this place must be a zoo in the morning." "Yes, but we like it that way!"

Ray was suspicious of some unrest and decided to push the issue. "Now why would 50-year-old store owners go to the trouble of making such renovations?" Stella got up and picked up a board. When she turned it around, the Duo read: GUN-SHOP FOR SALE. Elle gasped and blurted out, "NO." Ray was more diplomatic and asked why the shop was for sale. Sonny was hesitant but finally said, "it is a function of natural history, we have had our turn and it is time for someone else to take over now that we are approaching the Industrial Revolution and it is time to convert our firearms from black powder to smokeless powder."

There was a long pause till Stella broke the silence. "Let me elaborate. We have both been working in this business for 30 years and we are financially secure. We made these renovations to attract a buyer. This shop has a large modern apartment upstairs and we have a large inventory of new guns in storage compared to the 50 new rifles and 25 new handguns on display. Sonny is a master gunsmith who does research and development for Colt and would like to continue doing this if he didn't have to do action jobs, repair guns, or be a salesperson. So if we can find a buyer, we would move to a small house with an attached shed for Sonny to continue his work for Colt."

Ray was thinking and finally said, "would you mind saying what your asking price is?" Sonny said, "the shop and private apartment is listed by the town as $3,500, the stock on display is evaluated at $1,500 for rifles, and $500 for handguns. Miscellaneous stock at another $500. and a stockroom of new guns at $10,000." "Whoa, it takes a lot of guns to come up to $10,000." "We know, as we pay a high premium for insurance against theft, fire, or water damage. Come with us so we can show you our storage room."

Walking in the room they stood in a center walkway as Stella said, "everything on the left are new Black Powder guns and everything on the right are the new smokeless guns. As soon as a salesman has smokeless guns available, we buy them. The military has just adopted the 30-40 Krag rifle in smokeless powder, and so every gun manufacturer is rushing to convert black powder guns made of 'gunmetal,' to steel guns with varying percentages of carbon made to handle the higher pressures from smokeless powder. As of today, we have $10,000 invested in this room."

Ray asked, "these guns come from the eastern USA, how do you get them in this room?" "These double doors open to the enclosed boxcars. We are on a rail line for freight deliveries. That is why the town has evaluated our shop so high in value! But guns, ammo, and any supplies all come in by train, and the train workers even unload the cars, with a small tip of course, heh?" "So, unless my cyphering is off, $16,000 will buy this shop 'lock stock and barrel?'" "Not quite, I exclude my machine shop tools I use for Colt work but it includes all the tools a gunsmith needs to do action jobs, and repair firearms— plus it includes a state-of-the-art reloading center that takes too much time for me to utilize."

Ray asked for some time to speak to Elle. Stepping outside, Ray asked, "would this be a business that we could be happy operating between capers?" "Why of course, this would be a pleasure to work at since weeks can pass between our being needed by lawmen, but we do not have $16,000." "Elle, after two years on the bounty hunting trail, I have a lot more than $16,000 in my personal account." "But that is yours, not ours!" "Elle Belton, you will soon find out that what is mine is yours and vice versa." "Ray Cooper, I am not with you for your money. You know why I'm with you." "Say no more, kiss me and let's go inside and buy a gun-shop."

As the Duo entered, Stella was still holding the for-sale sign as Ray said, "we would like to make you an offer." As he wrote a bank draft he said, "for your asking price of $16,000 I tend this bank draft. In return for this amount we would like Stella to spend a month with Elle and teach her the business. I will spend a month with Sonny reviewing how to do action jobs, repair guns, and beef up guns for fanning or for better performance. I will not get involved with Colt research. Beyond the month, you will continue to live upstairs at no charge. Stella will then be partially retired as Sonny will be free to use the shop to do Colt research for a private fee and at his chosen schedule."

"Now the hook in all this, is that when we are gone to help a lawman with a problem, we can be gone from one to three days. Then is when Stella will come out of retirement to run the shop. We will also add another employee to help Stella and us on a full-time basis. Even when we are gone, Sonny will not be affected by our absence. When we are gone Stella's salary will be worked out but will be at least twice the Texas minimal wages." Elle then summarized by saying, "you get your price, sonny is free to do research at his chosen schedule, Stella is in partial retirement, and you get free rent for as long as you stay with us—and I'm going to be a total wreck till we get an answer from you!"

Stella looked at Sonny and said, "well dear, this is exactly what we asked for, plus we get to stay in our home and you get to do what you like, plus I get double minimal wages when I work. So, it is your choice, but if you agree, then break up this sign and put it in the stove." Sonny looked at the Duo and said, "would you consider hiring my younger easy-going brother who has been laid off from a competing gun-shop. He would be a general all-around experienced worker that won't need training and will fit in anywhere, especially when you are gone?"

"That sounds ideal, we would interview him as soon as we take ownership—that is if we buy you out." Sonny threw out a huge smile as he broke the sign up and said, "folks we have a deal." Stella asked when they wanted to start. Elle said, "how about in two days after we make a visit today to the town clerk to close the deal, and do some garment shopping and other purchases before we join you to learn the business."

*

After leaving the town clerk, they left with a signed bill of sale and all the signed paperwork to generate a new deed. The Duo then stopped at the bank. Ray stopped by the president's office and said, "I would like to transfer my personal account to the new business account by the name Cooper and Belton. President Willis stepped to the spare cashier slot and made the transfer. When Elle came to sign the transfer, she just about collapsed. A bit shaky, she managed to get her signature down and witnessed. After the private account was closed, the Duo thanked the president and left. Outside on the boardwalk Elle had to sit down on a bench. Eventually, she said, "Ray Cooper, why are you still risking your life doing capers and why purchase a gun-shop to make you work—you have $79,000 in the bank?" "Because money is not going to make us happy. Working together whether it is on a caper or selling guns is all part of life. We need to have a life, and just spending money is not a life. We can use money to make our life's paths smoother and it takes money to make money. With extra money we can make others' paths easier thru our charities."

Elle was mesmerized by his speech and suddenly got up and jumped into his arms as she melded to his lips and refused to let go until Ray picked her up and threw her on their buggy's seat. All the way home, the lovers held hands as Elle leaned her head on Ray's shoulder.

After making some fresh coffee, Elle asked why they didn't keep the upstairs apartment for themselves. Ray answered, "for several reasons. When gone out of town, it is wise to have the Greathouses upstairs; plus we need to be able to leave the store and travel the short mile to our home, where we fell in love. Over time we can add a windmill well, internal plumbing, a water closet with a toilet and a septic/leach field set up, as well as expanding the house as needed."

After a hot ground beef and gravy sandwich, the Duo enjoyed a fresh bakery raspberry pie. That evening the Duo sat in each other's arms as both were reading articles that Sonny gave them on smokeless powder, and how it was going to revolutionize the military and the commercial shooting industry.

After reading the articles Elle asked Ray what he thought of them. "Well, I just can't believe we won't need to clean our guns after shooting them and only do so when the mechanism is slow and or sticking." "Yes, that is true but how is that going to affect our business?" "It is clear to me that we will have to be careful who we sell smokeless ammo to since, if shot in an old gunmetal black powder gun, it will likely explode the firearm—it will require proof that they have a certified steel firearm to safely shoot smokeless ammo." "True, but in the storage area, did you see any smokeless ammo?" "No, plus there are new firearms that will fire some new calibers. The new calibers include: 38 special, 44 special, 30-30, and the old 45 Long Colt." "Wow, that is going to take some organization, especially the 45 Long Colt which will also come in black powder." "Yes again, plus wait till you see this new Winchester lever action model that fires a new 30-30 caliber bullet!"

Once they tabled the powder discussion, the Duo was beginning to get frisky. It didn't take long for their hands to start roaming. Suddenly Elle stopped and said, "why have you not touched me intimately. Even after I placed your hand on my breasts you did not attempt to go further. Are you hesitant because of my virginity? If so, just remember that virginity is a resolvable condition, not a contagious disease."

"Oh darling Elle, you have no idea how much I want to be intimate. I want to 'pleasure' you, but I don't want you to think it is a lustful response or a dutiful service under the sheets. I want it to be attentive to your needs, but I am slow to advance in the sexual graces—for it is my nature to need some encouragement!" "Well in that case, come with me."

Standing next to their floor mattress, the clothes started coming off. Once nude, Elle guided Ray's hand to her very private parts as he brought her hand to his manhood. "From now on, my love button and flower are free range." Once laying down Elle said, "pander me." The lovers started exploring their bodies cautiously, gently, but without hesitation.

Elle was the first to get overly excited. She knew she was experiencing a new pleasurable sensation which was getting unbearable. It was natural for things to progress. That is when she realized that a newfound event was about to unfold. It followed that her excited state started to peak and she started with uncontrollable contractions.

Elle held her breath, groaned, and followed with a loud yelp.

Panting to catch her breath, she finally started to speak between breaths. "Even if I live to be a hundred-years-old, I will never be able to describe what pleasurable event just happened." Ray then added, "I believe you just had an orgasm." "Well if that is what it was, does that mean that I am done for life?" "Oh no, a woman's response is like a church bell, it can be wrung over and over again, heh?"

After a long pause Elle asked how she could express the same feelings toward him. Ray gave some directions and Elle started her ministrations. Ray could not resist her magic fingers as he arched his back, groaned, and had an uncontrollable eruption. Elle was startled but quickly responded with continued stimulation while containing his milky seed.

Afterwards, things were different. The lovers were holding each other while whispering very private words and touching without restrictions. It continued for some time when suddenly, Elle's legs started shuddering and clearly her body went into another release. Without hesitation, Elle again proceeded to attend to Ray's needs.

The night was like a honeymoon for two consenting adults. By morning Ray had a dry release, and Elle was finally satiated. The lovers got up, drew a mutual bath, and then had their first replenishing breakfast. The talk during breakfast was about how they could simplify their lives when working each day plus be out of town on capers. It was Ray who said, "how about we add a windmill well, inside cold-water plumbing, a full water closet by combining the chamber pot closet and the utility closet, and add a septic tank/leach field. Later we could add a hot water boiler, central heat, and expand the cabin to three full bedrooms and an office." "Wow, I did not expect that answer, but why not? You said our money was to make life easier, and internal plumbing with a water closet sure makes this much easier. Plus, we do not need a chicken coop and 50 hens to care for. On our way to town we'll stop and see the Sanchez and we'll make them an offer they won't be able to refuse."

*

Arriving at the Sanchez's, the entire family was seen in their large garden. Elle started, "our lives are changing and we don't need a chicken coop and 50 hens, how would you like to own everything?" Beto said, "we'd love to have it with three teenage sons that eat like they are starving, but we cannot afford it." "No, you don't understand, take the hens, coop, and all the feed/bedding, and rebuild it on your land—free for the taking." "But Elle, we are proud Mexicans and must pay for it." "Then how about a dozen eggs left in the stable each week?" "Wow, that there is a heck of a Texas deal, thank you, and we'll start tearing the coop down today."

Arriving in town, the Duo went to see Elle's favorite carpenter. Durgin Stanton. After an hour-long discussion, the Duo left with a tentative contract to arrange for a windmill well, inside plumbing, a full water closet, septic system, and a full open-bedroom where the Murphy bed was located—all for a $2,000 deposit.

Their next stop was Harrison's garment store. Ray got some upgraded work clothes that matched Sonny's attire. Elle picked some tops and skirts and went into the changing room to try them on. Exiting the changing room to show Ray her attire, Ray was speechless but his smile said what his devious mind was thinking. Elle was quick to say, "keep it in your pants and save it for tonight, heh?"

The last stop was an office supply store. Elle realized that she needed to add a Remington typewriter, a Burroughs adding/multiplying machine, ledgers, and a multitude of office supplies. With three large boxes, several bags of new garments, work shoes, and more ;

the Duo had a full buggy and headed home to unpack and talk to the carpenters who had subcontracted for a windmill well. The remainder of the renovations would be done by Stanton's experienced carpenters.

***

CHAPTER 4

Learning the Business

That night was their last night before taking over the gun-shop. Picking up the garden vegetables, the Duo decided to keep the garden going by making it an evening project working together outside. Supper turned out to be meatloaf, garden peas, and mashed potatoes. The supper talk was about their anticipated day at the gun-shop. Elle was planning to watch Stella deal with customers as Ray was planning to follow Sonny's direction. After the dishes were done, the Duo set their floor mattress down with the bedding, and then sat on their sofa to watch their fireplace.

After their last night of liberal sexual freedom, the Duo never hesitated and were soon both nude on the sofa. Elle could see that she was responding quickly and took Ray's manhood in her hand to try to reach their nirvana simultaneously. When Elle started holding her breath, she started picking up her ministrations, and as she groaned, she heard a deep groan from her lover. For the first time, they reached a perfect nirvana simultaneously.

The Duo managed to pleasure themselves simultaneously a second time before sleep took over. Awake at dawn, the Duo decided to make it to the shop before anyone else so they could start the fire, make the coffee, and be open when the pastries were delivered. Allowing for coffee and doing their personal business, the Duo arrived at Enos's livery to put up their buggy and horse. By 8AM, they arrived at the shop only to find four customers enjoying coffee and pastries with Sonny and Stella.

Elle asked, "what time should we arrive if we want to open the place?" Sonny added, "I come downstairs at 7AM to start the fire and put the coffee on. The pastries are delivered at 7:30 and usually she is followed by some regular customers. Then we open the shop ready for business at 9AM and we close at 5PM sharp as we work thru lunch to serve the working class." That was when Ray said, "perfect, that gives us time to enjoy mornings at home and be here for 9AM."

Stella was ready and addressed the first customer with, "hello Sir, how may I help you?" Throughout the day Elle was taking notes. By noon, it had been a profitable sales morning. Stella had a sandwich to munch on along with coffee as a man appeared. "Hello Amos, glad you could make it. Elle, this is my brother-in-law." After the introduction, she went to get Ray out of the shop and all three walked next door to Dixie's. After placing their order, Ray said, "tell us about your past work history." "I have worked at a gun-shop in San Marcos for thirty years. Now that I am a widower, I quit my job and moved 20 miles to be closer to my brother and Stella. My best position is at the front desk selling firearms but can perform action jobs and can restock shelves when the need arises. In short, I can do whatever job you need done except fix broken guns. I have a nice apartment close to your shop and I'm willing to work full-time on a salary instead of hourly wages."

Elle said, "would you be willing to start at 10AM and work straight thru to closing at 5PM, even if the closing time drags out some days?" "Sure would." "Just so you know, Stella and Sonny are training us for the next month and there is no reason why you cannot start soon. Plus, if we disappear for days working for lawmen, then Stella and Sonny will be back to work along with you. When we are not gone on capers, we will work till 4PM to allow us to make bank deposits, order supplies, pay for old orders with telegraph vouchers, and do the necessary shopping for the shop and our own household."

"So I would be alone from 4PM till closing." "Yes, unless Sonny is working late on a Colt project." "But you don't know me, why would you trust me with the money and the office safe's combination?" "Because Sonny and Stella said so, heh?" "Then I would be honored to take this job." "But you don't know what your salary will be?" Well, my brother said you would be fair and I trust him." Ray said, the state's minimum wage is $13.50 a week for a six-day, 10-hour day. You'll be working a fixed 7-hour day, six days a week, but till closing which is unpredictable especially around holidays and vacations. Is $22 a week acceptable?" "More than fair. When do you want me to start?" "Two more days from today. By then, Elle and I should be ready to walk away from the sales desk to get familiar with the other jobs we'll have to learn."

*

The week went by quickly. The carpenters were busy at the house once the windmill well came thru with an adequate water supply. Amos showed up Saturday to learn the shop's unique methods and worked all day without pay just to be ready for Monday morning—of course Ray handed him a $20 double eagle gold coin before thanking him for his work ethic. That night the Duo went home to find the carpenters were loading up their tools.

Durgin said, "we are done and hope you will enjoy that new gas hot water heater, the gas lanterns, and the scullery utility sink, that were not part of the contract. I added them so I did not need to return you any money. So enjoy them and let me know when you want to expand the house. Oh, I forgot, we also added a gas heater in your so-called open bedroom and your new water closet."

Stepping in the house, all the changes were clearly visible including their mattress on the floor—but now in their bedroom. The real surprise was the water closet. Elle could not resist and had to flush the overhead toilet tank only to see the water rush to flush the toilet. Last of all, they had a four-legged porcelain tub made for two. With hot water in the faucet, the Duo filled it halfway and jumped in. After cleaning up, they added more hot water and lounged. Elle then said, "from now on, we draw our mutual bath and then have a nightly business meeting." "Well, we are here so let's review our past week and what lies ahead."

Elle started, "I have been the head salesperson for two days and I am very comfortable doing the job seeing how well informed I am about all the guns we are selling. Next week, I will learn the business aspect of keeping books, making payroll, placing orders, paying invoices, and keeping a ledger inventory. Once you learn that aspect, who will replace you if we get called into action. Amos would take care of sales and restocking shelves as Stella would help with sales, but also take over running the office with all its duties. Now what about you?"

"My past experiences have helped me get a hold of the gunsmith shop. I can dismantle any firearm, replace the broken parts, and then reassemble the firearm. It is not a mystery to me. Plus, Sonny got me involved in the storage room. I have studied the information manuals on every old and new firearm in storage. Plus he got me started with maintaining an inventory. Next week I am meeting with salesmen from Stevens, Winchester, Remington, Colt, Harrington Arms, Malcolm rifle scopes, Webley British guns to include the Bulldog revolver and the Greener shotgun. It is my hope we can set up an automatic delivery system for the commonly popular firearms according to last year's purchase history. Plus, we need to make arrangements to receive any smokeless rated firearm without ordering them; and as well as getting ammo for these new smokeless calibers. As a bonus Sonny invited the salesman for TEXAS LOAD in Dallas to a meeting. They are presently making casings for all the new smokeless calibers and will soon be loading them with smokeless powder as well as the new copper jacket bullets from Austin's TEXAS BULLET for the new 30-30 rifle caliber.

Elle added, "so if we don't start getting ammo for the smokeless rated firearms, we may need to start loading them ourselves?" "Correct!" As their meeting was coming to an end, Ray asked what the weekly sales had been. "The total deposits for a six-day week came to +- $2,000. With a 20 % markup, that leaves 10% for operating expenses, and 10 % for our profit." "Or a yearly profit of +- $10,000 a year." "Correct, and if we want to make more money we need to increase sales which means attracting other communities to shop for guns in our shop." "Correct!" Now, I am getting hungry, what do you say we get up and try on our new lounging outfits, the sweatpants and pullover sweatshirts."

*

Sunday they went to the Methodist Church to hear Pastor Genson. Afterwards, they stayed for the Sunday social in the cellar community hall. It was a luncheon followed by dancing. Elle made contact with her old schoolmates as the couple did their first two-step and waltz. Afterwards Ray got to meet these gal's beaus and or husbands. Before leaving, the Duo was invited to the local town hall for the weekly Saturday night dinner and dance. After they got home, they took their guns and went practicing in their own range. By morning, after extracurricular activities in their new bedroom, they were ready to tackle the week.

Elle walked into the shop's office, situated between the gunsmith shop and the walk around rifle displays, with a Remington typewriter, a Burroughs adding/ multiplying machine, a box of ledgers, and a box of miscellaneous office supplies. It was an intense lesson from the experienced older lady and the recently high school trained young gal. With a concerted effort, they blended their methods to create a realistic modern way of keeping the books.

Ray was informed by Sonny and Stella, that he was responsible for maintaining a storage room inventory, restocking the shelves, and placing orders on Elle's desk for her to process. As previously agreed upon, at 4PM the Duo left the shop to make the bank deposits, place telegram orders with payment vouchers, pay old invoices with telegram vouchers, pick up the mail, and do some shopping.

Each day Ray met with salesmen. In preparation for the scheduled visits, Ray had made a list of the firearms he wanted well stocked in the shop and storage room. The list included black powder firearms:

Winchester—single shot 22 bolt action rifles, Model 1886 lever action in 45-70 and 45-90, Model 1873 lever action in 44-40, Model 1887 lever action shotgun, and Model 1893 pump shotgun—both in 12-gauge.

Remington—The Model 95 derringer in 41 rimfire. The classic buffalo era 'rolling block' rifle in the modern 45-70 caliber and double barrel shotguns with or without external cocking hammers in long traditional barrels or coach guns. Choice of an ejector/extractor or just extractors.

Stevens—Single shot break open rifles in 22 long rifle (Crackshot), and break open single-or double-barrel shotguns.

Colt—Peacemaker revolver, Model 1892 DA revolver, Colt New Line SA 22 caliber revolvers, Model 1877 DA revolvers, Colt Mini revolvers (belly guns or storekeeper guns).

Webley—British dealer for the 41 rimfire DA Bulldog, and the Greener double barrel shotgun.

Harrington—The DA 22 long rifle revolver and the single shot Model 1871 break open rifle in 45-70/45-90 with ladder sights or a Malcolm scope known as the Classic Buffalo Gun.

Malcolm rifle scopes—the new short models such as the 18-inch long ¾ inch tube with a 6X power.

Ray met with every salesmen, and made it clear, "if we don't have your guns in the shop, we cannot sell them, heh? So keep them coming in and don't forget that they come from thousands of miles away and take two weeks to get here." Ray was able to set up a credit account as long as he maintained full payment within 30 days of delivery—and that included the firearms he was hoarding to get thru the hunting season and the Xmas holiday.

There were two salesmen that attracted Elle into the discussion. They had much to say about the coming smokeless era. Stan Bigelow from Winchester Arms made it clear that their new smokeless rifle, the model 1894 lever action 30-30, would likely be the first one to hit the commercial retail shelves. It was now in production and was made possible because of the new carbon steel barrels and receivers. Stan also admitted that it was a company ploy to hold off the production of ammo for these guns, but also admitted that there were several companies/foundries that were already making dies to load the new calibers to include 38 special, 44 special, and the 30-30."

The other issue was the popular 1873 rifle. "When we start converting this rifle to smokeless grade, it is planned to make it in the 44 special caliber to avoid mixing it with the 44-40 in black powder." As far as future offerings, Stan mentioned that a new pump shotgun was still in development but would be a major advancement over the present Model 1893 pump shotgun. This new model 1897 pump shotgun would revolutionize the shotgun industry.

On the same line Evan Crenshaw of Colt Industries had much to say about the expected changes. The first Colt firearm to be certified for smokeless powder would be the Peacemaker. His words were clear, "when you see that the cylinder retaining screw is being replaced with a spring-loaded base pin latch, then you will notice that the serial number will be over +- 170,000 and that a triangular stamp will appear over the top of the trigger guard with a VP stamped inside—Verified Proof."

Moving on he talked about the Model 1892 DA revolver and how it has been a disappointment. "As you know, Sonny has been working on changing the weak mechanism parts and is presently working on reversing the counter-clockwise cylinder rotation that is causing the lock-work to go out of time. We expect that each improvement will change the model from 92 to 94 and to 96. But we will not make this revolver into a smokeless rated firearm or in the new calibers. Instead Colt R&D is working on a new heavy duty DA revolver in hardened steel and in the new calibers of 38 special or 44 special. It will also have a roll out six shot cylinder with same funny looking grip and be called the Model 1898 New Service—that is an expected 'keeper.'"

Meeting with the Harrington salesman, Ray said, "as for the lineup, I use the SA six shot 22 revolver from Colt, but for an upgrade, your 'breakopen' DA six-shot revolver is a keeper. Now I have continued to keep your Buffalo Classic single shot 45-70 on the display shelf. With your new steel barrel with a microgroove rifling, it will become a tack driver for a copper jacketed 300-350 grain 45-70 bullet. With a new 6X scope, it will be a big bore long range gun for special hunts."

The Malcolm salesman was proud to demonstrate their new short 18-inch 6X rifle scope. Realizing that the new scope was a universal fit for any rifle, Ray gave the salesman a list of rifles to include a barrel mount and adjustment dials for each specific rifle. The list included:

Winchester lever actions, Model 1873, 1886, and 1894.
Remington Rolling Block.
Harrington Model 1871 break open rifle.

After the other salesmen left, Elle wanted to know why we would be doing more business with Winchester, Colt, and Stevens. Ray answered, "Winchester and Colt have all the popular state-of-the-art firearms, Stevens has quality guns at a very economical price. Plus all three companies have a salesman in Texas who oversees a distribution center right here in Texas. That means deliveries within 48-72 hours. All the others mean deliveries within two weeks from the east coast plants."

The last thing that was arranged with each salesman was a regular supply of firearms according to the statistics amassed by Stella over the past years. Extra orders would be the purchasing agent's responsibility.

*

That evening, in their mutual tub, the Duo had to make a decision. Elle said, " with our regular advertising we are selling $2,500 worth of guns and ammo each week—which comes to +-110 guns and ammo each week. Now I have an idea how we can push that up to $3,000 a week, but it would require more storage space and even another employee—a master of all jobs in a gun-shop from gunsmith, to salesman, to inventory manager." "I see, well what marketing ploy do you have in mind?"

"People buy guns for shooting pleasure, competition, self-defense, and hunting. Now pretend you were going deer hunting for the next two days and planning to stay over one night. What would you want to bring with you?" Ray pondered the question and finally said, "I would want some comforts of home, so I would bring a pup tent, a pot and pan to make coffee and heat up beans and bacon, and some privacy papers." "Is that all?" "Well other than my guns, ammo and a compass, yes, I guess?"

Elle had that impish smile as she asked, "what about a canteen for fresh water, how about a dragging cord, a hunting knife to field dress your kill, some beef jerky, a waterproof rain slicker, a multitool for a jammed gun, a wool blanket for cold nights, an extra wool sweater; just to name a few." "Wow, that is too much, I think I would just go for the day, travel lightly, and only bring the essentials." "Yes, a day hunt is much simpler but not as much fun, heh?" "So where is this going since you are like a law wrangler, you never ask a question without knowing the answer."

Elle hesitated but answered, "how about a day pack and an overnight pack—that is a hunting backpack?"

"Wow, what an excellent idea, so what is this going to cost us and can we afford to tack on our 20% markup?" That is all prepared and typed up for your approval, but first let's eat, I am starved." "But dear, as you can see I am ready for something else, heh?" "No time, after supper we still have to go over the list of each backpack items, before even considering bedtime activities."

After a fried chicken supper, the Duo went to work preparing a list of backpack contents.

Day pack

Small heavy cotton backpack.
Blanket insulated aluminum bottle canteen.
Privacy papers, dragging cord, skinning knife.
Rain slicker, multitool, medical kit/bandages.

TOTAL COST $11.00

Not included: Extra wool sweater, ammo, beef jerky, bedroll, and miscellaneous personal items.

Overnight pack

Extra-large heavy cotton backpack with bottom anchors for a tent.
All-inclusive day pack items.
One-man waterproof pup tent.
Small pot, pan, cooking griddle & eating utensils.

Not included: same as day pack exclusions plus bacon, coffee, canned beans, and premade sandwiches.

TOTAL COST $17.00

After seeing the contents and costs, Ray said, "this will be a service to our customers plus great items for ladies to make Xmas presents." Elle added, "and once in the shop, I am certain that we can coax them in buying a box of ammo!" To Elle's surprise, Ray grabbed his gal and was pulling down her sweatpants as he said, "I declare, the business meeting is adjourned and it is now time to make amends for holding me fully randy for an extra hour." "That can be arranged. But maybe you want to hear what Stella told me about 'safe sex?'" "Uh-uh, I know 'nutt-ting' about safe sex. So fire away, what is another few minutes in a holding pattern?"

"Well, I asked Stella why she had two kids and none more after that, and she said, that they practiced 'safe sex.' Elle went into all the details as per Stella's instructions. Afterwards, Ray said, "so we have four safe days a month to copulate freely, the remainder of the time is up to me to withdraw before brimming or we revert to our present way of making love." "Which is nothing to minimize, but you are likely correct in saying that once, like Adam and Eve, we taste of the forbidden fruit, that there will not be anyway of going back with satisfaction." "I'm afraid so, but for tonight, the old way is still a welcomed conjugal visit for two people in love and wishing to service each other's needs."

*

The next morning, Elle was again showing off a new outfit. Ray was awestruck and finally said, "you are naturally beautiful, plus your outfit brings out your female attributes and curves. No wonder you sell more guns than Amos or Stella. Why they line up to be your next customer at times when Amos is left twiddling his thumbs or becomes the cashier for your sales." "Well I can dress down if you wish?" "Yeah, with your mischievous impish tricks, you would likely step outside the house in your birthday suit." "True, but look at all the guns we would sell today, hey?"

Once at the shop, the Duo took a cup of coffee and went to their private office to plan their day. Amos came to the door and said that Sheriff Dolan wanted to have a word with them. Guiding the sheriff to the coffee pot and pastries, he said, "it has taken me longer than usual to collect all the telegraph vouchers on the Hollister and Humbolt gangs. Anyways, I sold everything and the total comes to $2,400 for horses, guns, and miscellaneous gear and $12,000 for bounties on 14 outlaws dead or alive." Ray pulled out $1,950 in cash and said, "$1,000 for the two Humbolt killers you put down and +- your 5% for the other bounty vouchers, and $250 for Deputy Crandall's warning of an outside Humbolt outlaw when he collapsed to the boardwalk with the classic 'thumping' noise. That should square us, heh?" "Sure does, now I have a business proposition for you."

Elle said, "and that is?" "Sheriff Burnside in San Marcos has been severely beaten by a group of extortionists who have taken over the town. Being alone in a town of 750 people, the US Marshal service is in no rush to give a helping hand. So for several weeks, the local merchants have been given the option of paying crooks for insurance, or risk having their businesses burnt to the ground or having the owner's wife assaulted. The sheriff can barely walk say nothing of trying to arrest these animals. Could you possibly take the train and see if you can put an end to these miscreant bullies who think they can roughshod mankind to their wishes. If you decide to take this caper on, I am certain that some of these outlaws will have a bounty on their heads. Plus, an extortion ring usually has three tiers of controllers. The guys doing the weekly collections are the wranglers who deliver their collections to the ramrod. Then the ramrod brings the collections to the head honcho, or the trail boss—a triple tier system just like on a cattle ranch, heh? And don't forget that this is the kind of thankless activity that will give you mileage as far as establishing your reputation beyond being a hired shootist or a 'Guillotined Lady,' heh?" Ray simply added, "as we told you, we'll help any lawman between Waco and San Antonio with anything they need help with—small or major threats."

Having three hours before the train departed for the 20-mile trip, the Duo stopped at the bank and started a private account for the telegraph bounty vouchers— again in both their names. They then went to the house to change and gather personal items, firearms, and Browny. At the railroad terminal, the head teller, Stanley Emerson, recognized the Duo and said, "your dog can be with you if he is behaved, or else he will need to go in the stock car. Also, take him outside to do his business during any of the coal/water stops; and I have pity for the outlaws you are going after"—with a smile he wished them a safe trip and outcome.

*

The train departed at noon and was in San Marcos 45 minutes later. To their surprise, an elderly man with a sheriff's badge was barely standing with two canes, had a face that was full of black and blue bruises, and a cast on his left hand. After introductions were made, Sheriff Burnside joked and said, "the only part of my body they didn't damage was my gun hand and my pizzle. But with a bum shoulder I can barely draw my gun, and the pizzle is on forced vacation till the swollen jewels go down and I can walk straight again—sorry for the dry humor!"

Needing to sit down, the Trio went next door to Wayne's Diner for lunch. While waiting for their order the sheriff explained how the extortionists were operating. "The owner of the Full Mug Saloon, sent for six thugs and sent them on a trial run. Each thug managed to punch a store owner as his buddy would assault the owner's wife by grabbing some very private female parts. They left with $10 and said they would be back once a week and to have the money ready. That was four weeks ago. The fee is now up to $30 a week and feared expected to keep going up. If any businessman hesitates, the wife suffers some sexual insult or the business loses a very expensive window."

Once the food arrived, the Trio enjoyed their fried chicken lunch. Afterwards, Elle said, "you said the ramrod has six thug wranglers. Where do the teams start their day?" "Team #1 is at George's Grocery, team #2 is at Butch's Butcher Shop, and team #3 is at Eleanora's

Haberdashery." "Fine, we'll be waiting for them tomorrow morning. Tonight we'll be at the Union Pacific Hotel."

After registering at the hotel, they had plenty of time on their hands. So they walked the main street and checked out the three mentioned businesses. Other than those three, the one business that caught their eye was a local gun-shop. The Duo went in and walked around to get an idea of how things were done in another town. That night, while dining in the hotel's restaurant, the Duo started discussing the two key things they found in the local gun-shop. The first was a nylon holster made in Colorado Springs at a local factory. It was durable, extremely light, and a size made for any handgun. They purchased one to get the address and full name of the manufacturer—Colorado Works. The other thing was ammo slides for rifle or handgun ammo that slid over the gunbelt or trouser belt. Ironically, they bought one to get the name and manufacturer's address—again Colorado Works from Colorado Springs.

That night, while bathing in their bridal suite, the Duo found themselves getting aroused. Elle asked if Ray was ready to try safe sex. After a long pause, he said, "I just cannot help but get randy just thinking of seeing you nude. Now look at me, hard as a stick and dripping. Why I wouldn't last a second without flooding you with my seed. Maybe we should wait till our first safe day, heh?" "Sure, but since we found each other my hormones have been so messed up that I have no idea when my monthly will finally arrive." "So, we can still pleasure ourselves, heh?"

The next morning after a rejuvenating breakfast of steak and eggs, plus one extra steak for Browny, the Duo was off to George's Grocery. When George was informed of their plan, he and his wife agreed to play along. As expected, two gunfighters appeared withing a half hour. George hands them the $30 but the usual receiver says, "the boss said it was $40 this week." George said, "well tell your boss that he can have the keys to the store, since $40 is my weekly profit and I am not about to work for nothing." Hearing George's comment, the other animal put his hand up the Missus's skirt as she slapped the animal in the face. The outlaw pulled his fist back when someone grabbed his fist. "Sir, a real man never hits a woman, but a woman can hit an animal for bad behavior; as Elle's butt plate smacked the man in the face to flatten his nose and bust out his two front teeth. Seeing the damage to his buddy, the other went for his gun as Browny grabbed a mouthful of the man's crotch. The man froze in place and turned white as a sheet with an open mouth drooling gobs of saliva. Ray was then busy applying manacles to their wrists and ankles as they were escorted outside, and somehow, the one with a sore "sac" tripped and fell face first in a pile of horse manure. Once both were secure to a water trough, the Duo went after their second team of ruffians.

The second team met the same resistance, Browny had grabbed a hand holding a gun and had eaten the trigger finger for breakfast. Elle had pounded the shotgun's steel butt plate onto an angry man's sac, and when he collapsed to the floor she managed to step on and crush one jewel to mush. Again, with both animals well secured to a water trough, they went looking for the last team.

To their surprise, a middle-aged lady was spread eagle and nude over a bed on display in the furniture store. Both animals were still stroking themselves to prepare to penetrate their victim. This time Ray jumped into action and from behind, booted their dangling sac of jewels with his steel toe work boots. Elle covered the lady and helped her get dressed. Ray manacled both men and managed to accidentally wrap their face against the store's front door frame. This time Browny was just an observer.

With the last team secured to a water trough, they walked right over to the Full Mug Saloon. When the barkeep directed them to Mister Rizzo's office, they met a 300-pound animal standing in the doorway. The man said, "need to see your appointment note, or go away!" This time Browny grabbed his gun hand while Elle popped him in the forehead with her trusted shotgun's steel butt plate. The result was that 300 pounds of meat acted like a stone falling in a pool of water. Once manacled, Ray yelled out, "anyone helping this man will get the same treatment."

Stepping inside the office, Rizzo was busy entering numbers in a ledger as he said, "who are you and what do you want?" Elle saw a flashy tool come down and pin the man's hand to the ledger. Rizzo was so shocked that he was speechless. Before he even said a word, Ray had an awl planted in a black rotten molar and Rizzo went stiff, wet and soiled himself. Browny was trying to cover his nose as Rizzo was moaning and screaming with every motion of the awl. To emphasize a continuing problem, the awl went thru another black molar and Rizzo passed out after suffering immeasurable pain. After joining the living, Ray asked him who the trail boss was and who was holding the loot. Rizzo said, "if you promise to put that pointed thing away, I will tell you."

Arriving at 12 Seymour Avenue, the sign read, "Noam Hoffman, Law Wrangler." Without knocking, the sheriff walked in and said, "we are here to arrest you for aggravated assault and extortion. I am certain you will enjoy your stay in the state penitentiary where they specialize in cornholing all new residents, especially law wranglers. Once the manacles were on, Elle said, "we want the money you stole from every merchant in town." "Go to hell," as he spit at her. Browny grabbed what appeared to be the man's pizzle as Elle said, "and the combination is?" "79-28-55. The steel box came from the merchants, and the rest is my personal income." Ray added, "the personal income will be restitution for the misery you caused, since you won't need the money in prison."

The next day, a US Marshal arrived by train to escort all eight extortionists to Austin for trial in a federal court. Several merchants had agreed to be witnesses. That same day, the Duo was packing their gear and were about to leave the hotel when Sheriff Burnside arrived for coffee and breakfast. "Well, I checked and all six wranglers were wanted for robbery, rape, and other crimes. I will gather the bounties, sell the horses and guns, and get telegram vouchers sent to your home address. Now, let me tell you of a serious abomination being carried on in our neighboring town of Killeen.

***

CHAPTER 5

Mixing Professions

Sheriff Burnside related the information he received by telegram. "Sheriff Sonnennoff has a rapist on the rampage. For six consecutive weeks, a working gal has been raped, sodomized, and been left unconscious in an alley. Things have just escalated to murder. The last and seventh victim was also killed by blunt trauma to the head. Of course, this last victim was the mayor's daughter. So there is a $5,000 reward for the capture of this animal. The real problem is that vigilante groups of three armed men are roaming the streets and any single man is stopped for questioning. As of this day, Sheriff Sonnennoff has his six jail cells full of suspects and District Judge Cunning has released all of them for lack of evidence—saying that walking alone at night is not a crime.

"Any idea what triggered the escalation to murder?" "Not sure except the dead victim was a local leader of the Suffrage League and was very vocal. Plus, the women in Killeen were recently allowed to speak at a local council meeting—which has angered many men!" Ray thought about this and finally said, "assuming that the local doctor has treated the six living victims and autopsied the last victim, we need to have a court order from Judge Cunning to obtain medical information from the local doc. If the sheriff got that court order, it would speed up the investigation." "I can arrange that, and when do you plan on arriving in Killeen?"

"Well it is 100 miles to Killeen and"......."And the next train leaves in an hour." "Ok, we are packed and we'll be on the train with Browny by then. On our way back, we'll stop and see how you are doing getting the last bunch of bounty vouchers." The sheriff thought, *"with the reputation they are building of making things happen, I suspect they may not be back for some time, especially with the trouble brewing next door in Waco."*

*

During their five-hour train ride, the train stopped twice for coal and water. On one stop, Browny had to visit the outside and find a friendly tree. To prevent traveling boredom, Elle asked, "what kind of animal would do such a thing to women, and to kill one, well I just don't understand." "This kind of behavior is from a deranged and angry man." "Does that mean he is mentally incompetent?" "Not necessarily, he is more likely mentally ill but knows he is doing illegal acts." "But if he is mentally ill, doesn't that mean that he'll not be found guilty?" "Oh, he'll be found guilty but will likely be sent to a mental institution till he is cured or if not, he will be a resident for the rest of his life. Now, always remember that this may be a case of a no-good killer outlaw who will hang when caught." "And it is up to us to figure out if it is a sick madman, or killer outlaw— plus identify the culprit, heh?"

Arriving at the terminal, a middle age lawman with an apparent young deputy were waiting on the platform. After introductions and adding Deputy Allen, the sheriff said, "you have reservations in the Killeen Queen Hotel, but not to rush you, I have the court order you requested and Doc Kilpatrick is waiting to see us tonight. If it is acceptable, Deputy Allen will take your dog, luggage, and long guns to your reserved suite as we walk two blocks to the doc's office?" "Very well sheriff, lead the way."

Entering the doc's office, they were greeted by a nurse who was introduced as the Doc's wife, Mildred. Escorted into the office, Doc Kilpatrick stood and extended his hand. "Welcome, I understand you have been tagged 'The Culminators' because you make things happen. Well, this abomination needs to have something happen." After reviewing the court order, the doc said, "where do you want to start?" Ray said, let's start with the living victims as we assume that you may have treated some."

"I treated all six. All six said the same story. They were surprised by a smelly masked man wearing a black walrus cap, who punched them in the left eye, and then everything went black. The next they recalled was to be found nude in an alley and dirty with semen all over them. Their exam revealed a large black eye, manually pulled pubic hairs, semen in the vagina and in the anal/rectum area. The virgins were vaginally torn up, and all had a ruptured anal sphincter requiring surgical repair." Elle was shocked and asked, "what about the dead seventh victim?"

All the previous findings were the same, plus the temporal portion of her head had been bashed in. I autopsied the head and found a massive bleed under the crushed skull as a cause of death." "What instrument was used in the bludgeoning?" "Not an instrument, but a human fist." Ray was taken back and asked, "are you saying this is misogyny at the extreme?" "No, more like the work of an angered incel."

The office exploded in questions that the sheriff clarified, "assume us normal people have no idea what you all are talking about. Please explain misogyny and incel." Ray proceeded, "misogyny is dislike, contempt, or prejudice for women. Whereas incel is an involuntary celibate man." Elle said, "are you saying they are bachelors that want to be involved with women but are not." "Close, these are men who have not been able to attract and establish a permanent sexual relationship with a woman. They tend to be mean men, scruffy and or ugly, ill-kempt, violent against women, often alcoholics, and a history of rape as a payback for women's denials."

The sheriff had been paying attention and finally said, "with the current ratio of one woman to six men or more, I suspect we may have several incels in town. How do we start looking for that one man who is violent compared to the law-abiding bachelors in town." Doc Kilpatrick said, "there is a unique feature in his semen?"

The doc said, "for you to appreciate what semen looks like under the microscope, look at this specimen. This is a healthy man. The sperm has a head with a nucleus of genetic material, a body, and a tail called the flagellum. In a fresh specimen, the sperm are moving in the semen, what the public calls the 'man's seed.' Now look at a sample of this incel's semen. Elle bent over the microscope and said, "I don't see any sperm like you had in the healthy specimen." "That is correct, this incel is sterile. This means he may have had the mumps as a young boy and that may have caused a case of orchitis which would have made him sterile." Ray bent down to look in the microscope and said, "I agree there is no sperm, but what are those bluish cells seen." "Those sir are malignant testicular cells. This man is dying of testicular cancer, likely a sequel of a severe orchitis many years ago. A physical exam of this man would confirm a testicular mass with evidence of spread to the inguinal nodes, or a swab of his urethra would confirm the malignant cells in a sperm free semen."

After the sheriff confirmed the same findings, Ray said, "and it is up to us to find this animal." Elle added, "but where do we start?" Doc Kilpatrick had had plenty of time to think about this and he finally said, "if it was me with a mass in that area I would seek medical attention in a populated city with a medical center—and that would be Waco some 60 miles from here. With that in mind, I sent a telegram to the head of the medical center that I often use and explained the need to identify a rapist and murderer. As a professional courtesy, I got this answer:

> Thank you for your medical search on the subject of aspermia and testicular cancer. We have had such an unusual case lately and the man's name was Declan Hammer. His last visit was two months ago and after he was given a terminal diagnosis, he disappeared and never returned to the clinic. I recollect that he was slim, some six feet tall, had a large scar from his left eye to his chin, and was generally scruffy and ill-kempt. I hope this was helpful.
>
> Respectfully DM McCutcheon, MD.

To finish their meeting, Elle asked how the first six victims were doing. His wife said, "it has been a humiliating ordeal for all six gals. These were professional ladies who were temporarily branded with a black eye that will take weeks to resolve. To make it worse, with the use of necessary stool softeners, these gals have to come to the office twice or three times a day for an anal power wash to maintain cleanliness for the sphincters to heal. Yet with our help, they will manage and get over this. At least none of these gals got the 'clap' and fortunately none of them will become pregnant, heh?"

With much to digest, the Duo retired to their suite. As usual, enjoying a mutual bath, Elle asked, "I know you have been thinking how we can catch this killer before he strikes again. So how long are you going to keep me in suspense?"

*

Ray finally responded. "There is no way we are ever going to catch this man in the act. Even if we start escorting every single gal home, it will take us weeks if we are ever successful. No, we have enough scientific evidence to get a judicial decision on the case. We just have to find him and confirm his malignant diagnosis and aspermia. But we have an emergency on our hands. This animal must know that his time is short and so I expect him to start accelerating his attacks." "Ok, so what can we say about him that will help us find him?" "Funny you should ask, but here is a mental list I have been working on: excluding their appearance as mentioned to Doc Kilpatrick:

1. He has plenty of money probably from a lifelong employment record.

2. He has an apartment for sleeping in but spends his days in a saloon.

3. He has his meals in the saloon and drinks beer all day.

4. He is a loner, and is not welcomed at private card tables.

5. So he plays solitaire or plays against the faro/blackjack dealers.

6. He does not flirt with the saloon gals as they do not offer their services just like a rooster does not play the field in the hen house.

7. In his back pocket or his apartment, he has a black bandana and a black walrus cap.

8. Being a walrus cap wearer, and likely of Irish descent, he probably worked laying rail tracks and has powerful muscular arms that account for knocking out his victims with a single punch to the face.

9. The bartenders are well aware of these types. But as paying customers, they do not say anything to the sheriff."

Elle added, "so that is where we start in the morning. Since there are three saloons in town, we'll need to spend time in each." "Yes, but probably not before lunch time, since these types are not early risers as they do their best work at night." "So, we have all night and plenty of time for a rejuvenating breakfast." "Yes dear, and do we start in the tub or on the bed?" "Try the tub for the first run, heh?"

Finding the sheriff in the hotel lobby, they invited him to the hotel's restaurant for breakfast. Waiting for their order, the sheriff asked what their next step was. Hearing their assessment, he suggested the only saloon that offered faro and blackjack to the customers without cribs for private services from saloon gals—Murphy's Saloon and Casino. The other two offered overnight rooms and personal services which an incel would not be interested in without privacy. With that in mind the Duo headed to Murphy's without Browny.

*

Elle sat outside the batwing doors as Ray went inside to have a chat with the barkeep. Stepping to the bar, Ray saw a name tag that said "Sam." To make small talk he said, "it appears that this is a universal bartender's name, why?" "That way troublemakers won't come out with a derogatory moniker and I can go home with some anonymity." "Ok Sam, I'll have a 'cold' beer for two bits. The beer was served as Ray took a gulp and had to pucker his lips to tolerate the cold liquid. Handing the barkeep his pay, the barkeep said, "it's two bits not a double eagle worth $20." "I also want some information!"

"Fire away for that price." "I am looking for an ill-kempt, scruffy, mean, loner, that smells. He drinks all day and will play the faro and blackjack tables since no one wants to play cards with him. Otherwise he may just play solitaire all day or evening." "Yes there is such a character that usually arrives in midafternoon. I end up serving him since the waitresses won't go near him." "Any special features?" "Oh yeah, he's got a scar on his left cheek from eye to mouth." "What kind of hat does he wear?" "A regular black cowboy hat, but you know something funny, sometimes he goes to the privy and leaves his hat on top of his table and cards—strange isn't it." "Well thanks for your help, and what does it take to reserve a chair at one of your regular poker tables?" "That double eagle was your reservation. I'll keep a spot for you, and I presume you want to be close to that hombre, heh?" This time, he hands Sam a single eagle and says, "why of course, direct visibility would be ideal!"

The Duo walked about the town boardwalk as Ray explained what Sam had said. Sitting on a park bench, Elle asked Ray how they should proceed. Ray was pensive as Elle said, "If we have the killer/rapist, we need to stop him tonight before someone else dies." "I know, but I am somewhat at a loss as to how we can catch him in the act—especially since he goes on a hunt but once a week, and that last victim was three days ago. We are going to do some serious long nights watching the streets and looking for that suspect."

Elle was perturbed, "Ray Cooper, it is clear to me that we need to entice him to go on a hunt so we can have witnesses as he attacks his victim—we need to entrap him to wear that walrus cap and appear with a black facemask—now face up to it. I am your partner and I am ready to do my part." "NO. you are the love of my life and there is no way I am placing you in harms' way. We'll come up with another method."

After a long pause, Elle said, "will you at least listen to this scenario?" "Listen I will, but no more than that!" "Ok, I will dress in that seductive gun-shop outfit that makes you randy all day—the one that shows my erectile nipples, plenty of cleavage, and tight jeans with plenty of lower cleavage and a prominent round bum. Along with this we will disguise the sheriff with a long beard, a disheveled plainsman hat, loose straggly clothes, a cane, and Browny at his side. The sheriff will be my witness as Browny will be my guard to bring down the scoundrel." "That sounds like a plan, but how will you prevent him from landing a round punch and flatten you to the boardwalk—a punch like that can kill you."

Elle had not set herself to fail when she said, "I guarantee you that that killer will find himself on the boardwalk writhing in pain and bleeding all over the boards." That is when she whispered something in Ray's ear that brought a smile to his face. "Well, lady, if that predator gets up to go to the privy after you leave the casino, I will follow him as another measure of security. Just remember what the other victims said, that they were walking the Main Street boardwalk when he appeared as an alley opened onto the boardwalk." To clinch the deal, Elle added the coup-de-grâce. She again whispered in Ray's ear and his reaction guaranteed that they had a plan of action.

*

Deputy Allen came rushing in and said that the suspect just entered Murphy's saloon. An hour later, Ray entered and was escorted to the empty chair where he could watch the suspect. After introductions, he started playing poker. Winning and losing, he appeared ahead when Elle made a dramatic entrance while holding the batwing doors open and standing there in her seductive outfit as everyone had stopped breathing to enjoy the sight. Spotting Ray, she said, "there you are darling!" Walking over she gave him a wet lingering kiss and said, "I am done with the investment meeting, and I am going back to our hotel." Picking up several $20 bills, she pocketed them as she said, "don't forget to wake me up when you come in, heh?" After she cleared the batwing doors, Ray said, "that's my gal and manager of our money. Ray tried not to laugh as the five other players were stunned by the show they had just had.

Without fanfare, the suspect took his cowboy hat off, stood, and turned about-face when Ray saw the black walrus cap sticking out of his back pocket. Ray excused himself from the next hand, and headed out the back door to the privy. To his surprise, the walrus cap wearer was walking behind the row of privies as he was heading down the street. Suddenly, he turned left into an alley. Ray took off on a dead run and knew he could be late and Elle might get clobbered.

At the same time, Elle was walking and paying attention to the alleys. She was prepared for an assault, as she could see the old man with a cane and a big brown dog on the boardwalk across the street. Suddenly, out of a momentary lapse of awareness, she saw an evil face standing within inches of her face, and a closed fist coming at her. In that moment, with her loaded derringer in her hand, she pulled the trigger thinking she was aiming at his groin. A loud smokey gunshot rang out as the suspect jumped up like a jack-in-the-box. By the time Ray, the sheriff, and Browny arrived, the culprit was still wearing his black face mask and walrus cap as he was thrashing on the floor and screaming to high heavens. Sheriff Sonnennoff unceremoniously applied manacles as he dragged the pathetic soul, hopping off one foot, towards the doc's office.

Arriving at Doc Kilpatrick's office, the prisoner was thrown onto the examining table. Ray was asked to pull off his boot with a hole in the boot top. During the rough boot yanking, the prisoner yelled and passed out. Elle quickly mentioned, "pull his trousers down, and check him for evidence of testicular cancer." While still unconscious, the doc did an exam and confirmed with enlarge inguinal nodes and a testicular mass that this was likely the rapist they were looking for. He then added, "we need a sample of his semen for making the killer Id" With the predator awakening, he yelled out, "hey, the problem is the hole in my foot. not my balls!" The doc added, "I am going to have to clean out detritus from your socks in the wound, and remove pieces of bones so you don't get a fatal infection. That is going to be painful and suggest we should give you some chloroform." "Nah, I am tough, so go ahead." Doc Kilpatrick grabbed the foot, did some poking in the hole with an instrument as the killer yelled to high heaven. "But I barely just started!" "Never mind, give me some chloroform."

Once under anesthesia, the doc donned some rubber gloves and turned the culprit on his side. The sheriff asked, "what are you doing, that's his butt hole, not his foot!" "I am milking his prostate, so put his member in the basin to catch a specimen. Elle was watching and was amazed at the male physiology. After the specimen was collected and placed under the microscope, the doc confirmed that we all had our guilty animal. After treating the gunshot, the rapist woke up none the wiser.

The next day an emergency conference was held between the Duo, the sheriff, the prosecutor, Judge Cunning, and Doc Kilpatrick. The prosecutor and Judge were given a course in male physiology and cancer, and verified the lack of sperm with an abundance of cancer cells. As the discussion started, the Judge wanted to know this man's life expectancy. Doc Kilpatrick said, "before he woke up I did an abdominal and general exam. His liver was enlarged and nodular in texture. I suspect he has less than three months to live."

After a long silence, the Judge said, "well it is up to you Durwood, are you bringing up charges on this man to call for a trial, or am I to rule as a special case that needs an executive judicial decision?" Durwood said, "irrelevant that this is a dying man, he committed murder in the most heinous way, and needs to pay for his crimes. As a judicial appointee and public servant, I have to do my duty, and I will prosecute without using the evidence obtained while the suspect was under anesthesia." Judge Cunning added, "that is a wise decision, for had I ruled on the matter, I would have sent him to the state penitentiary till he died of natural causes.

*

The trial was held two days later and the witnesses for the prosecution were Elle, Ray, and Doc Kilpatrick. He was found guilty on all charges and was hanged a day later on the town gallows.

After collecting their $5,000 reward they gave $500 to Doc Kilpatrick for his forensic help that led to the arrest. Looking forward to getting back home, Sheriff Sonnenhoff put a damper on their plans. Over a fresh cup of coffee, the sheriff explained how the legal system in Waco was corrupt and how merchants were robbing the people with abusive charges. A telegram came in from Deputy Sheriff Bill Thurston claiming that Sheriff Homestead was leading a rustling ring and several rustlers had been captured by ranchers and they all claimed that Sheriff Holmstead was the ringleader. Plus an honest hardware store owner, by the name of Winston Hicks, filed a complaint, with the District Court, of price gouging under duress by the League of Merchants. Judge Craymore has issued a bench warrant for the arrest of Sheriff Holmstead and the League leader, Isadore Tremblay. So as you can see, things are a mess."

Ray added, "sounds like a job for US Marshals. What goes there." "Apparently, the deputy can't arrest everybody by himself. The US Marshall service said it would be six weeks before they could send a clean-up crew, but if the local law arrested those under a bench warrant, the US Marshal would arrive to escort them by train to the county seat in Austin where the Federal Judge would conduct the trials." Elle added, "and if they wait for the clean-up crew then Sheriff Holmstead and Isadore Tremblay will be long gone out of Texas and with bags of money, heh?"

Ray added, "well we are willing to give the deputy a hand, but we need some authority to make arrests." "Apparently already covered, Judge Craymore will name you special district agents with a county badge to display.

He has even issued a $5,000 reward to whoever puts an end to the criminal activity and extortion that has gone unhampered for the past 8 weeks. With a nod, Ray said, "we need to get our gear in order and send some telegrams. We'll be on the noon train to Waco to travel 70 miles to our next destination.

The first telegram was to their gun-shop:

HEADING TO WACO, SHOULD BE DONE IN A WEEK STOP CAREFULLY CHECK OUT ANY INFO ARRIVING FROM COLORADO WORKS—WILL DECIDE LATER STOP HOPE TO BE BACK BY ONE WEEK Ray and Elle

The second telegram went to Colorado Works

WE OWN A GUN-SHOP IN NEW BRAUNFELS TEXAS STOP SAW A RECENT SAMPLE OF YOUR NYLON HOLSTERS AND YOUR AMMO SLIDES STOP PLEASE SEND US A CATALOG OF ALL YOUR PRODUCTS AS WELL AS A PRICE LIST PLUS ANY EXTRA INFO STOP

*

Two hours later, the train arrived in Waco. Deputy Thurston was waiting for them and invited them to the nearest diner for a cup of coffee and a chat. Ray started by saying, "we have been briefed and know what needs to be done. First of all, we need to take Sheriff Holmstead out of circulation." "Hold on, he now has 24-hour guards that are well known gunfighters, some of which are wanted 'dead or alive.'" "So noted, then we'll arrest this Isadore Tremblay." "Again, this one has three full time guards of the same genre and with no value for human life." "So noted, now where are the rustlers that were captured?" "Locked in a secret warehouse location and guarded by some reliable ranch hands." "Good, so after we arrest those two leaders, we will hold a meeting of every League Merchant member and explain what their restitution will be versus a lengthy stay in the territorial prison, heh?" "Yes Sir and Ma'am. And here are your special agent badges issued by the Judge as well as the bench arrest warrants for Holmstead, Tremblay, and bodyguards."

Bill followed the Duo and Browny to the sheriff's office. On the boardwalk a tall ill-kempt gunfighter stopped them. "Where in blazes are you going?" Ray spoke up, "we are here to arrest you, your other buddy, and that excuse for a sheriff." The gunfighter went for his gun as Elle said to Browny, "catch hand." Browny clamped his jaws on the hand holding the gun and the thumb and trigger finger were instantly amputated. With the gun on the boardwalk, Browny had a thumb and index finger for lunch. As he crunched the bones up, the gunfighter bellowed out with the most delayed expressive scream that shook the boardwalk. After shackles were applied, the Duo entered the office with the outlaw holding his truncated hand. Seeing Browny's work, the sheriff said, "get that cur out of here or Blackie will shoot him on the spot." Elle stepped up and said, "now Blackie you wouldn't do that would you?" "Like the boss said, out or I shoot him. Elle showed him that impish smile and without warning slammed the butt of her shotgun into Blackie's face. The upper lip was split in half and teeth were flying as the nose flattened. Poor old Blackie simply slid onto the floor.

Afterwards, the sheriff yells out, "I will have you arrested for assaulting my two guards as he went for his side arm. Elle yells out, "I wouldn't do that unless you would like to lose a thumb and trigger finger, as Browny was drooling all over the sheriff's desk. At the same time, Ray had the sheriff by the collar as he rammed a fist into the crooked lawman's nose and eyes. "I am arresting you for malfeasance, dereliction of duty and rustling. BAM another punch hit in the same spot. "Now, here you go into your own jail cell as Ray hurls him across the room and landed him on the cell's floor. "Get use to the bars, they'll be your solace compared to the team cornholing you'll get each day, heh?"

After jailing the two guards, the team made way to Tremblay's office in the League's private club. Setting foot in the club meant getting thru the doorman. A growling wolf-like creature gave the group passage. At Tremblay's door, another bodyguard was determined to prevent entry. When he went for a shoulder revolver, Browny took a solid bite on the guard's crotch. The guard looked like he had seen a ghost and was breathing hard while stuttering some blubbering words. When handed the manacles, he actually applied them himself, thankful to see Browny let go of his pizzle and sac.

While the deputy was taking custody of the guards, the Duo entered the private office. "I don't know how you got past my guard, but since you are in, who are you, and what do you want?" Without warning, a strange carpenter's tools went arched over the man's head as it ended its journey in Isadore's hand, now impaled on the desk. Isadore sat down, and started groaning as well as sweating bullets. "Take it out, take it out!" Elle just shook her head and Ray pulled it out but quickly shoved it into Isadore's mouth—heading for a black molar. Between teeth, Elle said, "we want the combination to your safe or Ray here will visit every rotten tooth you have and then I will cut your pizzle's cap off and make you shoot your load and pee sideways? Afterall we don't want to disfigure you to the public, heh."

After four teeth, wetting himself and moving his bowels, the stench was terrible and Browny, with his sensitive smell, had to leave. Isadore was spent and finally shed the combination 50-14-48. In the safe was $20,000 which accounted for overcharges made to local customers and out-of-town homesteaders and ranchers.

Three days later a meeting was set up in the town hall. All League Merchants were handed a personal invitation and warned they would be fined $2,000, per court order, if they failed to attend. There was a total of 20 League members and 100% attended the meeting.

Sitting League members at tables for four, the Duo and the newly appointed Sheriff Bill Thurston started the meeting. Ray said, "as a special appointed agent, I am legally bound to tell you that someone has filed a complaint against each of you/" There was laughter and snickering. Ray came back with, "you may think that is funny, but Judge Craymore does not and has labeled it a crime of greed against humanity—you have been PRICE GOUGHING! So, as of this moment, YOU ARE ALL UNDER ARREST." There was ranting and hollering as Elle put her hand up and added, "I know you are all armed, but if my wolfdog, who is roaming amongst you, sees one firearm pulled out, you will surely lose a thumb and trigger finger if not your entire hand."

Ray came back when the resistance quieted down. "In lieu of prison time, the Judge is willing to accept a monetary fine as restitution for your illegal acts. You have all charged your wares marked with a profit of 50% instead of the customary 10% profit margin. You owe that 40% surcharge as your fine." Elle then took over. "Today only, the fine will be $2,000 if you have sales over that profit level, but you must pay the fine of $2,000 today to Sheriff Thurston. For those of you who do not have sales in that profit range, take an appointment to meet with the judicial appointment accountant to pay the lesser fine based on your actual sales—and come with your business ledgers and your bank draft book."

Sheriff Thurston took over. "The fines will be deposited into a special account that I will dispense to townspeople, homesteaders, and ranchers who have been overcharged—bring your receipts or your credit booklet as proof of sales."

*

The next day, the Duo deposited the Judge's reward and the Duo packed to return home. After a quick lunch, they walked to the railroad terminal only to find the new sheriff waiting for them. Having a pleasant visit before their departure, Sheriff Thurston managed to say that there were counterfeit $5 bills appearing in Houston. Elle looked up and said, "that is a federal problem and the new federal secret service was established to resolve those issues—none of our concerns. We have been gone three weeks and have a business to attend to other than this Paladin crusade, heh?"

***

CHAPTER 6

Preparing for 1894

Arriving at the shop, the Duo was a bit surprised to see Sonny's sign down and a new one that said R & E Guns. Stepping inside Stella and Amos were pleased to see their bosses. Sonny also came out of his shop to greet the owners. After placing a sign in the shop entrance that said, "will open at 10AM today," everyone was ready for a meeting.

The first item of discussion was an introductory kit sent by Colorado Works. Stella and Amos had chosen holsters for all the handguns sold in the shop—both in nylon and economical leather. The order included all the accessories that were available. The extra holster was a speed shooting rig for the Colt 1892 DA roll out cylinder, with six-shot speed loaders and a special holster for six speed loaders and a clip-on pouch for empties.

The Duo looked at the $1,150 order and Ray smiled as he said, "nice choices, we'll place that order today." Elle then asked, "what else happened. Stella took a deep breath and finally said, "we kept Elle's schedule of advertisements, and to be blunt, we have been busier than is manageable. Amos and I have had to work overtime, and we even had to hire Sonny to help manage the storage room and repair guns." "Has everyone been paid time and a half overtime?" "Yes, money is not the answer, we need more permanent help. To make it worse, the only competing gun-shop in town closed down because of the owner's health. They ran a sale and sold all their new guns at cost, and we bought their used firearms at 30% of Sonny's evaluation."

There was a pause as Ray asked where help was needed. Amos said, "we need a fulltime storage room manager. I cannot be away from this customer service front desk for that is where the money is." Stella added, "you need a second salesperson between 10AM and 2PM daily and all-day Saturday. But don't look for a new body, for I would like to have this position. I like working here, but like to get up late and have play time with the girls during the afternoons." Sonny added, "eventually we'll need a gunsmith to do action jobs and repair firearms, as I am getting busy working for Colt and now Stevens.

As far as the office, if we had a purchasing agent and an office worker, we would function better when you are both gone on capers."

*

It was eight months later when the Duo was enjoying a hot mutual bath. After cleaning up, they added more hot water and just soaked to relax. Ray finally said, "how is Vicky Ross working out?" "Very well, she sees the work without being directed, prepares the daily deposits, and keeps a tight inventory working with Roger Musgrove to keep orders on track. She, along with Roger and me, now meet with the firearm salesmen and has complete control in making and paying for orders—old and new. I get the feeling that Roger is also doing his job well?" "Yes, he was a quick learner, knows when an item is selling faster than usual, and is busy all day now that we expanded the storage room by 100% and doubled the long gun displays as well as the glassed handgun displays."

Ray then asked, "does Archie Dunsmore help out in sales?" "Oh yes, and he watches the waiting lines and will come out of the shop when he sees customers waiting to be served." "Great, well he is a master at repairing firearms and he makes twice his daily wages with just action jobs or repairs. Plus when Roger needs help to

unload a rail boxcar, he is always there to help him out."
"Well then, what is next on the marketing agenda?"

"The day and overnight backpack kits will soon be a reality and way ahead of the hunting season. Vicky is negotiating with a warehouse in Galveston that is supplying mail order sporting goods companies and many gun-shops. The goods come by freight ships from the east coast. We are expecting samples of every item we had placed on the day backpack and overnight backpack. Once we approve each item, establish our individual cost, add our 20% markup, we'll set up a display, and open up sales."

"I see we have weekly sales up to $2,500. Why is that? We are a gun-shop in a small town. It doesn't seem realistic." "Well Stella believes that men are coming from out of town to see 'The Guillotine Lady!'" "Oh well speaking of that, lately we haven't had much action in that line of work." "Why is that?" "Guess, the lawmen are doing a better job or people are content with their income and the crime rate is kept low. I suspect that the local lawmen will have trouble handling kidnappings and or wife beatings. I suspect we'll get calls for those sooner or later."

"Other than 'The Guillotine Lady,' what else has attracted outside customers?" "There is no doubt, it is the lightweight nylon holsters. Why men show up with a firearm and match it to the nylon holster size. Ladies show up requesting a nylon holster for a specific handgun, and want it giftwrapped. We are already on our third order at a 20% profit and the bestselling ones are: a small 22 pistol for the killing coup-de-grâce, the ever-popular derringer, or the handy shopkeeper mini-Colt revolver."

After a long pause, Elle said, "I am beginning to think like you do. The problem with that is that I know what you are thinking. As lovers we want what our mate wants and so I know you are somewhat disenchanted with the gun-shop. Why?" "Oh no, I love that shop. It's just that since we hired and trained our staff, made improvements, and added new lines; there is nothing for me to do these days. I have even thought of opening another shop in Austin. some 50 miles away, to take advantage of the large population, but I am comfortable living where we are, and I am not interested in working away from our home." "I see, well the next big thing in gun sales is the smokeless era but that is still a year away since we don't have any smokeless ammo yet."

Ray, again pausing, Elle finally said, "we'd better get dressed, grab a quick supper, and put the hot water on, we'll need some strong coffee and a strong back to deal with the visitors we are expecting tonight. It all started with our neighbor, Drummond Caswell, coming to visit me at the gun-shop today. All I know is that he said he would make us an offer we would not be able to refuse!"

*

The Caswells arrived and Elle introduced them to Ray and added, . "these folks have been our neighbors since I was a child, and my dad and I have hunted his woods for years while harvesting a deer twice a year." Drummond added, "and these woods are what brings us here." Looking serious, while addressing both, he added, "how would you like to be MILLIONAIRES in eight years?" Ray nearly slid down his lounging chair as he said, "whoa, I feel like a mule that just got clobbered on the head with a 2X4—you have our undivided attention. Tell us more!"

Drummond started, "for three generations, we have owned 5,000 acres. Half is pastureland and half is a forest. My grandfather spent a lifetime harvesting timber on that woodlot and finished 60 years ago. Since then my father and I have been ranchers as the forest re-grew. In my grandfather's golden years, he would spend his days in the woodlot cutting away less valuable seedlings. So today we have a timber lot that is 60-70 years old and some of the firs are dying off. It is time for a profitable harvest as most of the trees are 24-30 inches on the stump."

Ray asked, "what kind of trees are included?" "85% softwoods and 15% hardwoods. To be more specific the softwoods are a scattering of pine, fir, and spruces. The hardwoods are mostly oaks. The major pine is Ponderosa Pine but it also includes some loblolly and long leaf pine. The firs are mostly Douglas Fir and the spruces include White Spruce, Colorado Spruce, and Red Spruce. The oak includes White Oak and Live Oak." Elle added, "I assume the softwood was for construction framing lumber and boards, as the oak would be to make furniture, cabinets, and firewood from the waste." "Correct!"

Elle asked, "I've always wondered why you maintained a fence to keep cattle out. "My dad learned years ago that cattle like the forest for the shade, wild grasses, and a place to hide to give birth. Well, that lead to dead birthing cows which we couldn't find so the fence went up." Ray was impatient and said, "so where is this leading?"

Drummond added, "we are ready to retire, move into town with some luxury living, but cannot find a buyer for the woodlot. We have sold the 4 sections of pastureland to our neighbor at $3 an acre, but no one has the funds to buy the woodlot or build a sawmill." "Assuming one was found, how would you make a living and a profit?"

Drummond said, "follow me and mark these numbers down. The woodlot is 4 sections or +-2,500 acres. Since there are 50 trees per acre, that means there are 125,000 trees. Now keep in mind that most 12-inch diameter trees yield 250 board feet (BF) of lumber, but as I have said, these trees are 24-30 inch on the stump. So each tree now yields 500 board feet (BF) of milled lumber. So 500 BF X 125,000 trees = 62.5Million BF." "So far so good?" "Yes." "Now let's talk money. Timber logs in the yard sell for $20 a thousand BF, whereas milling a thousand BF adds another $15 for a total cost of $35 a thousand BF. It doesn't take a math genius to compute (62.5M ÷ 1,000 X 35) equals 1.9 million dollars. Say half for land, equipment, and labor and the other half for profit!" "Wow, and you said in eight years?" "Yes, I have already computed that 10 men on a modern mill can saw 25,000 BF in a 10-hour day. Then multiply by 300 workdays a year etc. etc. and etc. as it comes to eight years."

There was a pause as Elle gave Ray the nod. "Well let's go back to investment costs." "The county agent has evaluated the woodlot at $6 to $9 an acre. We would be satisfied with $6 an acre." Elle said, "really, that comes to $15,000 for 2,500 acres." "True, but it includes 50 acres north of the buildings to build a sawmill plant, and all the buildings that include a two bedroom house that can serve as an office, a 15-man bunkhouse with a separate kitchen, a windmill well with a 500 gallon concrete tank, inside plumbing, plus a 30 stall barn that will need to be converted to stalls that can handle draft horses for lumbering and some for private smaller traveling horses. Plus the hayloft has a year's supply of this years' first cut hay and straw."

"Alright, now let's talk about the costs involved in building a sawmill plant." "First some history, in the past most sawmills were water powered which required being on a sizeable river. Today the modern sawmill is steam powered by a wood boiler on the premises. This allows dry land installations. Now I can breakdown each cost for the mill, a drying shed, a sawdust bin, a bark shed, a boiler, two chain conveyors, hundreds of feet of roller ramps, concrete platforms, and many other accessories too many to mention; or I can give you a package price that includes everything possible to make a sawmill plant excluding the hydraulic gas tractor to move logs about the yard and onto the mill."

Ray added, "I like packages that take the planning out of the equation. How much. "$10,000 and you'll be able to fire up the boiler for your first day of milling." To the Caswell's surprise, Elle and Ray never flinched. Elle broke the silence and said, "can Ray and I step outside for a moment?" "Certainly, take your time, this is a big investment."

Walking away from the house, Elle asked, "could this satisfy your yearn to be totally involved in a project?" "Yes, but will you run the gun-shop while I spend my days at this endeavor?" "No way, I have spent 20 years of my life finding a man, and I am not spending a single day not being with you. I can do the work of a man, and will be at your side each day, or FORGET IT!" "Well, we likely can spell you or me, one afternoon a week, to check on the gun-shop, and the rest of the time we will become sawmill owner/operators, heh?" "And on the road to become millionaires."

Stepping inside, Elle said, what is the company that provides the sawmill plant package?" "That is 'Woody's Engineering' out of Tulsa, Oklahoma." Elle writes out two drafts as the Missus nearly collapsed. Drummond then added, "I take it, it is a go?" Ray acknowledged it and everyone shook hands on the deal. Then Ray said, "now please tell us why you chose this company's steam operated mill over others?" "Well here are my seventeen reasons:

1. 500 miles to Tulsa, versus 1,300 miles to the Carolinas, or 1,200 miles to Hill City, South Dakota or 2,000 miles to Portland, Oregon.
2. The actual sawmill is delivered in pre-assembled large pieces.
3. There is a sequential numbering for oiling pistons, wells, and grease taps.
4. The technician sets up the mill and the steam generator; then will spend the rest of the week verifying that everything is working properly.
5. It includes a map of the entire 30-acre plant layout.
6. It includes 20 spare parts that are likely to need replacement.
7. Overnight freight delivery of breakdown parts to avoid milling down- time.
8. Five-year warranty on the boiler and certain milling parts, and 100% warranty on the entire plant for two years.
9. Two chain conveyors to the sawdust bin and the chip shed.
10. Built in steel brush log cleaner.
11. Built in edging/ripping saw with side mini-crosscut saw.
12. Engine oil injector to mix oil with steam.

13. Governor to maintain plant's rpm.

14. Shed and building blueprints to include: concrete platforms, sawmill overhead steel roof, elevated sawdust bins for auto bottom loading, chip open roofed shed, extra-large drying shed, and elevated roller ramps for loading logs onto steel brush cleaner.

15. Miscellaneous, waste bins on wheels, sawdust/ chip barrels on wheels, slab racks on wheels, elevated rollers to the drying shed.

16. Recently added. All sawmills in the past year have had a woodchipper added. I know very little about this, but you will get to see it in operation.

17. And the best for last, it includes a 30-day course at the Houston College of Applied Sciences on the science of timber milling plus applied training on a Woody Sawmill—and it does have a woodchipper. Tuition is free, but housing and meals are your responsibility."

There was silence in the room as Drummond handed the Duo two textbooks on "Everything you need to know before milling lumber." and the two actual brochures on the Woody Sawmill. It was Ray who then added, "so we need to hire a carpenter/clerk of the works, buy a gasoline tractor and get it modified to lift logs, and make arrangements with Houston to register and be trained to operate a Woody Sawmill, heh?" "Correct, and it has been a pleasure to do business with you. See you tomorrow at the town clerk's office and then we'll order a Woody Sawmill."

*

The next morning, after their usual replenishing breakfast and bath to wipe off the sexual sweat, the Duo started at the shop to tell them of their changes. Fortunately none of the workers were surprised except that everyone agreed that a shop manager needed to be named. The Duo agreed to do so after their return from Houston. Next was a telegram to Houston College asking for the next available spot on the Woody Sawmill program. Then the Duo went to see Stanton Construction. Durgin looked at the multiple blueprints and the plant layout and said he could be the clerk of the works and could get this built up during their stay in Houston. Durgin pointed out something interesting. The only building that would be finished was the one covering the sawmill. All other structures would be built out of green framing lumber milled at their own sawmill and roofed with galvanized sheets. To get this project started, they had to find lumberjacks, a cookie, a barn wrangler, and some draft horses.

Fortunately the Caswell cookie and wrangler had not been hired by the new rancher, so the Duo quickly filled those two spots. Advertisements went in all local papers to include San Marcos and Austin. Waiting replies from the ads and the Houston College, the Duo went out looking for a gas-powered hydraulic lift/tractor and draft horses. Enos Rutledge at the livery found three matched teams of four-year-old Belgian Draft horses for $1,500 with fitted harnesses plus his finder's fee of $60.

Heading to Maitland's heavy equipment, the Duo found a prototype gasoline powered tractor already equipped with a front-end bucket that was convertible to front-end forks depending on the job. The asking price was $1,000. With full payment it was delivered to the Caswell site the same day.

Checking with the telegraph office, they had a telegram from Houston College. The answer said that the next class would be held in one week and only two spots were left out of a possible 10 students. The Duo quickly sent a $200 deposit to hold their spot and agreed to arrive next Saturday for registration and preparations for Monday classes.

*

The weekdays seemed to slowly pass by. The Duo both read the textbooks twice, studied the diagrams on the Woody Sawmill's brochure, watched the Stanton carpenters lay down concrete and even practiced driving the gas-powered tractor. As the day approached their departure, Ray said to Durgin, "go ahead and buy some green framing lumber and build all the buildings so we can operate when we return from Houston. Just get the roof over the sawmill done since the manufacturer confirmed they would be arriving with the sawmill in ten days."

The last thing that was scheduled were interviews for lumberjack and experienced sawmill workers. It was a long day at the town hall when interviews started. After hours, they had chosen ten experienced lumberjacks and one older horseman to drag out the cut logs. Another hour later they had accumulated another eight experienced sawmill workers—one with heavy equipment experience. After preparation time, Ray started the joint meeting. "At any point, if you cannot live with the work conditions, please take your leave since this is not a job for you."

1. If you are out of town, we expect you to move to town. No one left.

2. Single men will live in the bunkhouse. Married men will make their own arrangements. No one left.

3. Pay for everyone is $5 a day for a 10-hour day, six days a week. Four applicants left.

4. Benefits include medical/accidental insurance and room and board for bunkhouse residents. If providing your own room and board, we will pay an extra $8 a week to help defray the expense, which is also the going rate for a single man in a boarding house. Two applicants left.

5. The cookie has control of the kitchen and the bunkhouse rules. No one left.

6. The lumberjacks will have a working foreman elected by the workers. No one left.

7. Every millworker will rotate on a daily basis to any yard job.

8. Trained personnel will operate the main circular saw, the steam generator, the edging saw, the crosscut saw, and the woodchipper. No one left.

The Duo was pleased to see that they had hired 6 lumberjacks, one field wrangler, 4 sawmill workers, and one tractor operator. The sawmill workers would start upon their return from Houston, but the lumberjacks were to start immediately to start stockpiling logs ready for milling.

*

Taking the overnight train to Houston, the Duo slept away the 175 miles and arrived at 9AM at the Houston terminal. Getting up for the last breakfast, Elle said, "I cannot believe we are going back to school. When we started work at the gun-shop it was clear that a diploma over high school was not needed since experience, brains, and hard work would suffice." Ray added, "but this time we need to learn a trade, and that is what trade colleges are for. We won't care for grades, we are students to learn how to operate the trade efficiently and safely, heh? What we learn in the next month will last us a lifetime."

A taxi brought them and their luggage to the admissions building where they met President Winthrop. After introductions and pleasantries, the president said, "let's go over the rules of engagement.

1. Couples' housing will cost $110 which includes free use of the pool and three meals a day.

2. The accepted attire in the sawmill is body fitting denim jeans, short sleeve shirts, some form of headgear, work shoes, and leather gloves. The men generally wear walrus caps with very short hair below the cap's rim. The ladies usually have a short haircut, but as an alternative, can wear an extra-large kerchief to enclose the long hair. These kerchiefs and caps are available in the campus store. In this line, you both have an appointment with the campus hairdresser at 3PM for the cut you desire.

3. In the campus store, you can also buy snacks, proper attire for the Saturday night banquets/dances, and the approved swimwear.

4. In your paid tuition, you are also getting two books. One is a textbook that the professor will follow plus a manual for the Woody sawmill. These are available in the campus store.

5. Your day starts at 9AM with classroom time till 11AM. Then you have an hour for lunch as the sawmill lab starts at noon till 5PM.

6. Personal protection other than hair covering, includes safety glasses and ear protection. These are included in the sawmill lab. It only takes a wood chip in the eye to blind you and the high

pitch whine of saws will eventually make you deaf. But your professor will discuss this with you."

"That does it for now. Any questions?" Elle said, "yes, why so much attention to short hair?" "The sawmill puts wood dust and particles in the air which are highly combustible. With hot metals or a spark, and bad luck, you will all suffer a spontaneous combustion/explosion which will startle you and singe any exposed hair. You won't let that happen again without your hair well covered. Anyways, get your meal tickets at the cafeteria, visit the campus store, the swimming pool, unpack your luggage in apartment 6, and be at the hairdresser at 3PM. You are then free till Monday AM."

*

The Duo was impressed with the outdoor pool as well as the barely clad ladies. At the campus store, they purchased work and dancing clothes, headgear, swimming trunks and snacks/cookies to include peanut butter, bread, and coffee.

Waiting for their turn at the hairdressers, Elle was frantically trying to hide her bushy long hair under the extra-large kerchief, but to no avail. Then a couple was walking out. The man had a nearly shaved head below the walrus cap's rim and the gal had a gorgeous short haircut that resembled the new style called a "bob cut." Ray said, "I like the man's cut, I'm getting it." Elle then looked at Ray and asked, "will you allow me to get a haircut like that gal has?" "Yes, you will always be beautiful to me no matter the haircut." After introductions, the Duo had just met their first acquaintance—Jim Ward and Jessica Stanley of Tulsa.

Ray went in first, wore his walrus cap and got the cut that was standard in the wood working labs. Elle did the same, and ended with what the hairdresser called a "utility bob." With the hairdresser's help, Elle learned how to wrap and tie the kerchief to hide 90% of her short haircut. Stepping outside, Elle asked, "do you still love me?" Ray whispered, "ridiculous, why of course, as long as you didn't include a 'bob cut' of your lower triangle, heh?"

After unpacking, the Duo went to supper. There they again met Jim and Jessica and had a nice chat. Afterwards, Jessica mentioned that they were going to the pool since the banquet was cancelled tonight because of construction. Agreeing to meet them there, the Duo went to their apartment to change. Demonstrating Elle's suit, Ray said, "Oh dear, your brown hairs are sticking out beyond the crotch edges, you need an edging shave."

"Are you sure or is it just for you to get your nose near my female parts?" "Dear, I've been there, now strip while I whip up some lather and strop my razor blade."

Wearing matching tops, the Duo was in style. Elle was showing plenty of cleavage and barely hiding lower brown hairs, but so was every other woman in the pool area. The Duo enjoyed bobbing in the pool with floats as they talked with Jim and Jessica. During the bobbing session another couple with the same hairdo showed up and joined their bobbing circle. The new couple was Ed Crenshaw and Sue Burbanks. Jim and Jessica were from Tulsa and had no plans of ever settling down in the lawless Oklahoma but also did not want the cold lumber states of Oregon, Washington, and South Dakota. Whereas Ed and Sue were from the cold country of Portland, Oregon, and they also had no plans of living in that cold country for the rest of their lives.

After a refreshing time at the pool, the three couples said goodnight and agreed to meet in the AM for breakfast. Entering their apartment, Ray was all over Elle. Finally she asked, "what has taken over you?" "I just realized that you were the most voluptuous woman at the pool. I am so lucky I could eat you." "Well don't let me stop you!" That was Elle's fatal mistake. Ray took her at her word and went ahead. Elle was a bit shocked but before she had time to object at the goings on, she started her climb and had a massive orgasm as she had ever experienced. Needless to say, Elle found the way to reciprocate her appreciation.

*

It had been a night to remember as both had experienced complete relations during her two safe days. The Duo then experienced the use of a shower to bathe and shampoo their hair. In time, they arrived at the church services where they saw the two other milling couples. Afterwards, they gathered at the cafeteria for a traditional Sunday hot lunch. Sitting and talking, Jim asked what there was to do on Sundays while on campus. Ed answered, "when we arrived I had the chance to talk to the last milling graduates. I found out that the instructor, Byron Lewellen, had pushed the class thru six busy days a week for the month, and Sunday was their only day of rest. To relax the milling students all gathered at the pool on Sunday afternoon. So Sue and I, being from the cold country, enjoy the heated pool and we plan to spend our Sunday afternoons at the pool." It took little discussion to find the other two couples would follow suit.

The topic that afternoon, while sunbathing, was about the showers in the student housing. Ed again said, "those are for us milling students who come home smelling like a sawdust bin. Standing to shampoo and rinse hair, and to rub/soap the sawdust off their skin, was best done by a shower compared to the old sit-down tub." Jessica added, "I love it for those reasons and a few others I can conjure, heh?" After laughs, Elle said, "gosh, don't give Ray more ideas, he's already innovative enough as it is!" And so the attitude of using pleasant realities amidst friends was firmly established. For the rest of the day, all six wondered what things would be like come morning.

*

Sitting in the classroom, the Triplets met the other two couples. Both were from Seattle and made it clear that they would return to their hometown after the month's instructions. Waiting came to an end when a 30-year-old man popped thru the door and said, "good morning, my name is Byron Lewellen, and I will be your classroom teacher and sawmill instructor for the next 24 days."

"I have prepared topics to cover each day and try to match the day's experience in the sawmill. Today is introductory time and I will cover safety and show you how this mill operates three major saws, a log carriage, one chipper, and two chain conveyors—all off one steam generator and one steam engine. So let us talk about safety and as I will explain later, take your work shoes off and place them tied together in the box. The campus cobbler will make alterations while we have our class."

"You have all been exposed to short hair, short sleeves, tight trousers, head gear, and leather working gloves. Now add ear plugs with earmuffs or the whine of the saws will make you deaf. Also, choose a pair of safety glasses with a folding case. These are necessary, for a wild woodchip can blind you in an eye for life. And finally, sawdust makes concrete like a skating rink. Even if it is etched, the sawdust will fill the cracks and you will slip if you are wearing smooth leather soles. That is why the cobbler is adding full width cleats from toes to heels to each of your work shoes. For working around saws and gears is not the place to slip and fall, heh?"

Without questions, Byron moved on to the next subject. "Lubrication. This sawmill has 30 sites that require oil wells to be filled, grease taps to be topped, pistons to be oiled, and pillow blocks to be oiled to keep mandrels cool. Each day five of you will each be assigned six lubrication sites labeled, 1-6, 7-12, 13-18, 19-24, 25-30. Of course we'll be rotating these so you will all have to memorize where the 30 sites are located." A few questions were asked in regard to the dangers of missing a lubrication point. Byron said, "a hot spot can ignite the sawdust in the air, and that is not something to want to frequently experience. Also, this process has to be repeated after the midday break for the afternoon run. The lubrication lasts 5 hours max, and 4 hours is much wiser." With no further questions, the instructor closed the class. "See you after lunch! Oh by the way, your 'cleated shoes' are in the box outside the classroom door!"

Going to the cafeteria, the guys wore their walrus caps as the gals had kerchiefs to hide 90% of their head. Apparently smelling of sawdust, since the sawmill was in the same area as their classroom, several other students sarcastically said, "so you are 'woodhicks,' heh?" Elle did not appreciate the attitude and the sarcasm as she stepped into the arrogant student's face and said, "Sir, woodhicks are lumberjacks. We are workers that mill logs into lumber and our moniker is 'millers.' So if you are going to insult us, at least use the correct nickname. We may smell of sawdust, but the sawdust smell is the 'smell of money.' Besides in eight years we will be millionaires—can you top that before you fall off your golden pedestal?"

After a cold meatloaf sandwich the class arrived at the sawmill. Byron was just firing up the boiler while he showed the students how to properly oil and grease their sites. "So you don't forget, follow the numbers in proper sequence assigned to you." When everyone was squared away, Byron opened the valve and powered the engine. He then went to every saw or conveyor and showed how the plant was powered, how each moving part was secured, and how each saw had protective guides to minimize injuries. It took all afternoon to explain each mandrel, steel plates, gears, paper pulleys, the carriage clutch with the to-and-fro action, plus the rack-and-pinion set ups to convert rotary to linear motion.

With the sawmill closed down Byron said, "tonight review the parts we showed you on page 1-4 of the sawmill manual, and read your textbook's Chapter 2 on the steam generator and the steam engine."

And so a pattern of classroom subject, followed by the applied sawmill paces, as well as nighttime reading, was well established.

***

CHAPTER 7

Houston College

The first night in their student housing apartment became a routine. First was the joint shower with plenty of roaming hands, and often reaching accidental culmination. Then to the cafeteria for supper and discussing their day with their friends. Then private time in their parlor reading their nightly assignments and taking notes of specifics that could be used in the future. By 9PM, the Duo was off to bed for their precious private time. That morning, they agreed that they would stick to light breakfasts and lunches, with only a full course meal at supper. Their breakfast consisted of toast, peanut butter, jam, and coffee. Their lunches would be a cold sandwich, two cookies, and coffee.

The class started on time. "The steam generator is the life of the sawmill. The operator has to arrive one hour ahead of the proposed work time to start the system making steam. First of all, add water to the half mark in this visible water tube, then start a fire with chips, sawdust, and kindling. Once started, add waste wood and slab-wood to get a good fire in the boiler. When the psi gets up to 150 it is time to slowly open the valve to the 45-horsepower steam engine. Drain all the water out of the engine to prevent an explosion of the safety valve, and then start the engine at a slow idle to warm up the piston and the attached gears while maintaining a pressure of +-125 psi in the boiler."

Ray asked, "I thought the steam engine was originally 25-horsepower. Why the change?" "1890 modernizations when the crosscut, edging, chipper, two chain conveyors, a bark cleaner, the newly added small crosscut saw next to the edger to cut 'stickers' at 4 feet that fit in the drying room racks, and last an overhead saw for timber diameters over 24 inches." Byron then explained how the steam engine works. "There is a steam chamber ahead and behind the piston. Filling each chamber consecutively makes it have a force forward and backwards. The more steam is delivered to the chambers, the faster the engine turns the master wheel which is attached to the main sawmill wheel with a four-foot-long belt. Of course to maintain the engine speed, the boiler pressure must hold at 125 psi, and an occasional peak at 150 psi is still safe."

Jim asked, "at what psi does a riveted boiler explode?" "I would never let it go as high as 225 psi without opening the blow off valve." When the questions ran out, Byron addressed how to lubricate the engine piston. "The number one position in the lubricating sequence is to add oil to the atomizer reservoir. This reservoir deals with each drop of oil by atomizing it and mixing it with steam. As long as that reservoir has oil; the steam engine piston is being lubricated."

Ray was curious, "I understand that the boiler psi should be kept at +- 125. But what are the rpms generated at these pressures?" "The steam engine is turning the wheel at 250 rpm, whereas with a 2-1 ratio, the sawmill rpms are at 500."

Elle then asked, "as often as I read about the sawmill's governor, I am still not clear as to what those darn balls manage to achieve. Can you explain this thing so I can understand it?" "Sure, that has to be the easiest question I ever get," as he fakes crying. "Here goes, when there is an excessive load on the steam engine, the rpms fall below 250 and the sawmill slows down. An example of that is when the main saw works its way thru a 24-inch log. Now with the strain on the engine, the centrifugal force increases and the three balls extend outwards which increases the steam to the engine to pick up the engine rpms. Vice versa, when the load goes down, the balls fall back toward center and the steam flow to the engine slows down to decrease the rpms. Clear as mud, heh? "Well it is getting better but still a long way to go." "Ok, well after lunch, I will demonstrate the 10 positions that each of you must learn in order to maintain a functioning sawmill."

The afternoon was well organized with several other instructors manning the stations that Byron was not demonstrating. By five o'clock, he had covered every station's duties. He then said, "tonight review out of the textbook, the duties you saw demonstrated, and try to remember what you need to do. The list of duties is on page 29 as I will again review with you."

1. "Steam plant operator, fireman, psi watchman, engine monitor.
2. Main sawyer with carriage operator, log roller, and saw placement.
3. Crosscut operator and stacking 24-inch slabs.
4. Edging saw operator, to produce four foot 1-inch stickers and eight foot 2-inch batten.
5. Lumber stacker.

6. Chipper operator for all waste wood.
7. Bark steel brush sweeper as prep work before sawing.
8. Lumber expediter to drying shed and stacking assistant.
9. Cleanup worker to include: assistant log mover and roller, pickup all waste wood and bring to chipper especially barked discarded stickers, sweeping floor of sawdust and other debris, and transferring waste bins to the boiler furnace.
10. Floor supervisor. The busiest job in the plant. Be ready to catch safety violations, assist all workers if they get behind, and seemingly always be on the lookout for hot bearings or picking up stray bark and sawdust which could be a cause of spontaneous combustion. Temporary replacement for workers needing a privy break and the immediate day replacement of a sick worker."

"As you can see, every job in this plant requires alertness, focus, and intent to do the job as efficiently as possible while maintaining safety—and that is why sawmill workers get the big bucks, heh?" With loud applause, the class was dismissed.

*

The next morning Byron shocked everyone as he said, "I have been informed that a couple owns a large 70-year-old/2,500-acre woodlot and is presently installing a sawmill plant the same brand as in our lab. So, since I know that location, many of my future classes will reflect that location. With that in mind, let's talk about the softwood timber that is found in southeast and southwest Texas. Please take notes!""''

"The three kinds of softwoods include firs, spruce and pines."

FIRS: "Except for a scattering of minor species, 95% of firs in this region are Douglas Fir. It is a strong wood and best used for framing or weight bearing spans. The wood is light brown with touches of yellow and red between growth rings. The bark of large trees has a grey or brown color and is deeply furrowed to make it a very thick bark—up to 4-inches or more. Sticky resin eruptions known as pitch (wet or dry) are common."

SPRUCE: "There are three varieties: White, Colorado, and Red Spruce. All three are strong woods and best used for framing but can also be used in making boards. All three species have a creamy white color with a scattered hint of yellow. 'Scaly bark' is classic of all three species. Some pitch eruptions are seen but not as frequent as firs.

WHITE: The bark is grey-brown with loose scales.

COLORADO: Similar to White Spruce but with shallow furrows.

RED: The bark tends to be reddish-brown."

PINES: "Pines in general are usually a form of brown mixed with other colors. Large trees have furrowed and thick bark. The wood is generally white with dark rings and very dark frequent knots. Bark scales are also a classic feature as well as deep furrows. The bark varies as follows:

PONDEROSA: Large trees are brown to black and yellow appears in very old trees. Scales are common as are deep irregular furrows.

LOBLOLLY: Red to grey-brown bark. Scales are rounded and in plates.

WHITE: Also red to grey-brown. The scales are layered and in blocks.

LONG LEAF: This tree has red-brown bark that turns orange with age. The scales are paper thin and the bark, like Douglas Fir can be very thick."

There was a long pause as many notes had been taken since this info was not in the textbook. Byron saw the confusion and finally said, "I know it sounds confusing and there are too many similarities. But when you are running the main saw, you will see what I meant and you will be able to see that the visual appearance of a log's bark and wood color matches your notes."

"Moving on, let's talk about board feet. I will only say it once; a 'BOARD FOOT IS A 1-INCH-THICK BOARD MEASURING 12-INCH WIDE AND 12-INCH LONG.' Is there anyone who disagrees with me?" Without dissention, Byron continued. "That same board, if it was 8 feet long would contain 8 board feet (BF) of wood. If it was 12 feet long it would contain 12 BF. Now take a six-inch board and it would be half of the 12-inch board, and a 2X6 would be the same as a 12-inch board.

Does anyone want to dispute those facts?" Without disagreements Byron said, "then read this chart, study it, and memorize it. Why, because one day you will have to scale an order of differing width and lengths and you either will be fair to you and your customer or someone will get screwed."

BOARD FOOT CHART

Size	8-foot	12-foot	16-foot
1X2	1 1/3	2	2 2/3
1X4	2 2/3	4	5 1/3
1X6	4	6	8
1X8	5 1/3	8	10 2/3
1X10	6 2/3	10	13 1/3

1X12	8	12	16
2X4	5 1/3	8	10 2/3
2X6	8	12	16
2X8	10 2/3	16	21 1/3
2X10	13 1/3	20	26 2/3
2X12	16	24	32

The classroom was quiet like a church during the weekday afternoons. Finally, with a smile, Byron said, "other than memorizing this chart, you can use the equation and determine what an odd size of lumber will yield in board feet. The equation is:

> Thickness in inches X by width in inches X length in feet and all divided by 12 = board feet. Take a 10-inch-wide two-inch thick board that is 16 feet long—2X10X16 ÷ 12 = 26 2/3 board feet (BF)

"The more you study this chart, the clearer it will become and by the end of the month, you will become scaling experts since you will be dealing with these dimensions from day to day. Get some lunch and this afternoon you will be running the sawmill as you will change jobs every hour till you become familiar with all of them."

*

The walk to the cafeteria was a continuous banter between students trying to figure out who owned a woodlot and was installing a state-of-the-art sawmill. It was Jessica who got suspicious of the Duo being rather quiet. Pointing at the Duo, she said, "there has to be a story behind that, and it will occupy our lunch hour before we get all the facts, heh?"

Fortunately, the Duo could alternate speaking so they could eat their egg salad sandwich and coffee. At the end, Jim shocked everyone by jokingly asking, "well, are you looking for trained workers, at the 'big bucks' wages Byron mentioned?" Elle threw it right back by saying, "well most likely, heh?" Ray even set the hook deeper when he said, "we haven't had time, but we need to prepare an employee package to include housing, wages, vacations, and benefits."

The afternoon was exhilarating. For the first time, every student had hands-on experience to half the positions and the other half would be covered on Friday afternoon before the weekend. Arriving at their apartment, the Duo was flying high since they had both had their turn controlling the log carriage and setting the main saw thickness and speed. With a tight embrace, Elle said, "what a thrill, there is no doubt we chose the right trade. I still see the boards falling free of the log and I don't think I can resist your hand in my pants much longer. Without a word, Elle unbuttoned his fly and took hold of his firm member. In no time both participants could no longer hold back and both experienced a mutual nirvana. Still standing in their parlor, Ray said, "once back home, if operating the carriage/saw causes such a response, I don't think we'll be able to get home without having an orgasm in our buggy. We'd better get over the novelty of it, heh?" "We will, but let's not rush it, heh?"

The next morning, Byron's subject was air drying lumber. "There is no doubt that fresh timber can be cut, sawed into framing lumber, and be put up immediately. The rest of the lumber has to dry. The way to achieve this is to separate each board or framing lumber by one inch, and add one-inch stickers to separate each layer. That way, each piece of lumber is surrounded by air. The time to achieve dry wood is one year as long as there is a roof over the stacked lumber to prevent rainwater from soaking the drying wood. As a matter of organization, place 4-inch-wide boards with 4-inch boards—do not mix. In addition, stack the 8-footers with 8-footers as well. So if a customer wants 12-foot-long boards that are 8-inch wide, they will be in their own stacks."

Ray asked, "so it will be a year before we draw a penny on this year's milled wood?" "Yes." "So how does a mill owner make payroll and other expenses." "By advertising and selling green framing lumber at a market discount. You may even generate a small profit this first year!"

"Speaking of payroll and income, let's finish our morning with a discussion of wages, work hours, safe working environment, and employee benefits. To start, let me say that I heard some instructors say, 'the only way to make money is to work 10 hours a day six days a week,' Well let me say that I do not believe this. To start, what is the number one cause of down time in any plant?—ACCIDENTS."

SO

"The #1 cause of accidents is—FATIGUE."

SO

"What is causing worker fatigue?—long working hours without time off."

SO

"Long hours = fatigue = accidents = disabled workers = lower profits."

"It doesn't take a genius mechanical engineer to figure out that the best solution is to work 8 hours a day five days a week and work every other Saturday at time and a half—that is the currently accepted norm for most industries as long as the wages are consistent for trained workers employed in a dangerous industry."

"In closing, please remember there is no money that can compensate for a lost limb because of worker fatigue. A word to the wise should suffice, heh?" Ed and Jim both noticed the Duo's double nod.

The day was finished with the last of the station instructions. As the class was leaving Byron said, "tomorrow, you will all spend 45 minutes at each combined stations supervised by an experienced instructor.

*

Saturday turned out to be a revelation. Having worked all seven hours, the closing whistle sounded at 4PM. Everyone appeared exhausted and had clearly experienced reality. Byron made things worse by saying, "now can you imagine doing this for 10 hours six days a week? Anyways, you have one hour to clean up and get dressed for the first dinner dance at the campus hall. Belinda and I will reserve a table for you, so try to arrive by 5PM."

The evening passed like a whirlwind. The Duo really got to know their coworkers. Everyone could dance the two-step and the waltz, and everyone was in a good mood. Elle admitted she enjoyed the friendship that was brewing between her, Sue, and Jessica. Ray felt a camaraderie with Jim and Ed that was natural and not pressured. The real shock was when the three gals went to the ladies' room. Jim and Ed were very clear when they asked if they could apply for a job in the Duo's new plant. Ray never hesitated when he said, "without a doubt, that can be arranged, besides do you think we would ever get those three gals separated? Let Elle and I get a package together and we will talk again but with the gals next time, heh?"

That evening, Ray confided in Elle about Jim and Ed's request for employment. Elle's response was such that their night was one to always remember—a thankful and happy woman, is a generous and loving bedmate.

The next morning, after an obligatory replenishing breakfast at home, the Duo stopped at the campus telegraph office to send a gram and voucher to Durgin Stanton in New Braunfels. Changes were requested and the funds were included to cover the expenses. Per their Sunday routine, they went to 11AM church services followed by Sunday lunch in the cafeteria. Their afternoon was spent at the pool with the two other couples—now the group was called the "Triplets." This being their third session in the sun, everyone was showing a tan along their swimwear attire. When they got home, the Duo went into their shower to rinse off the pool chemicals. Yet the Duo never got out of the shower without each reaching a shattering orgasm after using every possible stimulation they could think of—as experience was no longer lacking.

*

The second week became the template for the next three weeks. Byron always had one or two topics for class time, and the afternoon was spent working the different positions in the mill. As was expected, each student was developing a favorite position. Realizing that Byron might run out of subjects for class time, the students started their own list to include favorite positions vs. rotating positions, salaries, and minimal benefits.

"Today's topic is saws: the main circular, edging, two crosscuts, and chipper blades. Saws are made of carbon steel with a Brinell Hardness in the range of +- 400-600 depending on the amount of 'coke' added as a source of carbon. They have to be hard to maintain a cutting edge, but still pliable to bend instead of breaking off when too hard and brittle. The specifics of each saw and chipper blades are similar, so here are the circular saw specifics:"

1. "The 48-inch circular saw has 40 teeth. The edging/stripping saw has 24, and the crosscut saws have 60 teeth. Most chippers have four 4-inch vertical and horizontal blades on an 8-inch flat wheel.

2. The main blade is 1/8 inch thick, whereas the teeth are angled out 10 degrees to make the kerf wider than the blade. By moving "in and out' alternating teeth 1/16 of an inch, the kerf will be ¼ inch wide.

3. When the cutting kerf widens, the teeth have to be brought in or twisted straight to maintain a ¼ inch kerf.

4. There are three parts to a tooth. The cutting edge, the back angle or the 'rakers' as they are called, and the gullet. The gullet is the wide part tween each tooth where sawdust is temporarily caught during the cutting process. To sharpen a saw, each part has to be filed down using a tooled gauge and a file that is harder steel than the

saw blade. There is also a 10-degree gauge to maintain the proper tooth orientation.

5. Keep pitch off the main blade or it will stick to the wood, heat up the blade, and increase the steam engine's load. Use pitch remover or standard dish soap to keep the saws clean.

6. There is a 24-inch top sawblade to be used when a log is larger than half of the regular circular saw—or 24 inches for a 48-inch saw.

7. All blades follow the 'rule of three.' That means that three teeth are in continuous direct contact with the wood to make the cuts. That is built in every circular saw depending on the saw's diameter and number of teeth."

After a pause, Byron asked, "Any questions?" Elle asked, "this % of carbon eludes me. What % carbon will produce a saw with a Brinell Hardness (BH) of say +- 600 compared to a file with a BH of +- 750." "An estimate would be 1.4% carbon for the 600 BH, and 1.8% carbon for the BH of 750."

Ray followed, "which worker or workers do we assign to sharpen saws?" "NO ONE. This is the kind of job that sawmill workers should not be doing these days when time is money. You need a retired machine shop worker who wants extra income, or use a sharpening shed. No one has the time or expertise to do a reproducible sharpening job. As long as you have at least two spare saws for each working saw, you can wait for the sharpened saws to return to the mill. Let's take a coffee break and then I will discuss dimensional lumber during the second hour."

*

"Dimensional lumber is the wave of the future. There is money to be made with a 33% advantage to the sawmill. Even if you discount dimensional lumber by 13%, there is still a 20% advantage to the sawmill over full thickness rough cut lumber. To review, a 2X4 becomes 1 ½ X 3 ½ inches. A 2X6 becomes 1 ½ X 5 1/2. inches. However larger lumber are different. A 2X8 becomes 1 ½ X7 ¼. A 2X10 becomes 1 ½ X 9 ¼. And a 2X12 becomes 1 ½ X 11 ¼."

"At current trends, half of the 2X4 are dimensional as one quarter of 2X6 are dimensional. 2 X 8 or larger are full thickness, as all boards are full thickness of one inch. The ratios will change as the demand changes. The key to a good sawyer is the ability to determine if the diameter of a log can yield an extra or more pieces of dimensional lumber or whether it is not worth it. I have charts that have made those determinations so keep a copy for yourselves. I will elaborate on the 'perfect sawyer,' later heh?"

"Any questions?" "Yes, how does a worker determine the board feet in a specific order of dimensional lumber?" "Simple, all lumber is full thickness when it comes to board feet determination—another advantage for the sawmill, heh?" "Ok, let's go for lunch and then spend the day milling Ponderosa Pine!"

The afternoon went smoothly till the main circular saw hit a spike nail. The nail had been overgrown with wood and had likely been driven into the tree by a hunter wanting to hang his jacket to dry. The saw's clutch was activated, and locked in place with a padlock that only the supervisor had the key. The saw was exchanged and a note left for the sharpening team in the machine shop. That evening, the Duo was reading ahead and covered the next days' topic.

"This morning let's talk about sawdust fires and spontaneous combustion. Sawdust bins notoriously catch on fire. If the delivery chute is moved to the next of three bins every two hours, there is a very low chance of a bin fire—especially if the recently filled bin is raked to flatten the layer of fresh sawdust over maintaining a high peak. In case of a bin fire, pop open the bottom trap door and let the burning sawdust fall to the ground where it can be watered down."

"Woodchips are high in bark content which means a highly volatile pitch content. This byproduct is best kept far away on a concrete platform covered with a high steel roof. Several times a day, the tractor with its front-end forks will manipulate the pile to dissipate internal heat. Keep in mind that the boiler operator is the fireman who chooses his three fuels to keep the fire going—sawdust, woodchips, and wood/bark slabs. All three if not used in the boiler are sellable products. A woodchip fire is simply hosed down and or disrupted with the tractor's front-end forks."

"Now spontaneous combustion is the result of carelessness. A sawmill has sawdust in the air that is not visible. Just look at the dust on your safety glasses and you'll understand what I mean. The fire is a flash explosion all over the sawmill and can result in singeing hair, clothing, eyebrows, lashes, and first-degree skin burns. The usual cause is a static electricity spark or a red-hot oily gear or bearing. The latter is correctable by paying attention. The static problem is manageable. Never wear woolen clothing, make sure that all steel frames and equipment are grounded to a bare copper wire that goes to the ground, or de-electrify your body by touching a grounded wire several times a day. The individual that triggers a spontaneous flash usually suffers the most damage including second-degree burns. Other preventive measures include wiping dripping oily parts dry, avoid smoking in the sawmill, and hope for a breeze that keeps replacing dusty air." Without questions, the class took their coffee break and then Byron started the second hour.

"What makes the carriage operator a true sawyer?
"It is a multifunctional second sense. Here are some examples:

1. A sawyer will look at the diameter of a log and will be able to tell whether it is most economical to produce dimensional framing lumber, or full thickness framing lumber, or one-inch boards.
2. He will be clear that the saw positions must vary by ¼ inch and include 2, 4 ¼, 6 ½, 8 ¾, and 11 as they vary the same with one-inch boards.
3. Can select non-standard length boards to make 4-foot stacking stickers.
4. Will always notice that the kerf is widening and time to change saws.
5. Knows how to mill 12 and 16 foot logs to get the maximum yield out of differing diameters in the

same logs. Any log that quickly drops its diameter will often end up in 2-inch batten, stickers, or narrow 4-inch- wide boards to secure rafters before steel sheeting is applied.

6. Will always wait for help in rotating a log a quarter turn before the securing 'dogs' are applied.

7. Knows when to ask for a break, and utilize the supervisor freely."

8. Has committed all the charts to memory that are used by the main sawyer.

9. Is astute and focused enough to watch not only the work at hand but the general overall function of the entire sawmill—especially safety violations."

*

The afternoon was going smoothly when all of a sudden there was a loud crack and a bright white light blinded all the workers. As a response, the boiler operator immediately disconnected the steam engine and all operations came to a halt. Every worker had a comment, some of which were profanities, but most were a questioning word and look at who or what was the culprit. There in plain sight was Byron, wearing a woolen cap, with an index finger touching a steel frame, but with the copper wire out of the ground. With everyone slightly perturbed, he said, "you should be lucky that today was a breezy day with the air dust somewhat low. Had there been no breeze, some of you would have landed on your butts and suffered widespread singeing and skin burns. I had to do it so you could appreciate what a flash burn can do." To continue the irritation, the mill went back to full operation till 5PM.

The next morning, Byron said, "today we'll discuss how to keep saw blades from getting dull. Basically it is a matter of clearing the dirt and stones from the bark since there are no debarkers yet available. The yard workers who prepare logs will scrape the large portions of stones and dirt accumulated from dragging logs thru the dirt. Fortunately the proximal portion is lifted off a wheeled axle and chained to it so only the back end of a log needs cleaning."

"The problem is large Douglas Fir and pines that have thick coarse bark with deep furrows. Of course the furrows need manually scraping with a pointed tool. Then the log is rolled under the steel brushes. These include wide rolling steel brushes that clean the bark's surface while narrow brushes clean the depth of the furrows. One pass under the brushes cleans one third of the log, so two more passes are needed before applying the ice tongs and winching the log to the holding area for the main circular saw carriage."

The second week came to an end as the workers were finally gaining some real physical endurance, and the job started to become a comfortable routine. The Duo found time to send a telegram to Durgin and asked for a status report. His report was thorough and read as follows:

PLUMBER HAS ADDED 3 BOILERS AND 3 SHOWERS STOP

NEW BUILDING AND SAWMILL SHED IS COMPLETED STOP

LUMBERJACKS ARE FILLING YOUR CONCRETE PADS STOP LOGS ARE AMAZINGLY CLEAN DESPITE SEASON STOP

TECHNICIAN HAS INSTALLED SAWMILL STOP

WILL RETURN UPON YOUR ARRIVAL STOP TO CONFIRM PROPER OPERATIONS STOP

CARPENTERS ARE NOW BUILDING DRYING SHED-WOOD CHIP SHED-SAWDUST BINS-PRIVATE OFFICE STOP

QUESTION—PHONE SERVICE ARRIVING NEXT WEEK STOP

DO YOU WANT FOUR INSTALLATIONS STOP

SHOP OFFICE-HOME-TWO RENTALS RSVP STOP

The Duo's answer was:

FOUR PHONES OK STOP
ADD A SHARPENING SHED WITH BENCHES-VISES STOP
ADD ANYTHING ELSE YOU FEEL NECESSARY STOP
TWO WEEKS TO GO STOP

It was Sunday afternoon and the Duo was getting ready for the pool when there was a knock at the door. It was the Quad that entered. Jim said, "you said we should talk again when the gals were with us. Well we are all here and we wish to know if we have a place in your sawmill operation?" Elle started by saying, "I have never had girlfriends till now, and Sue and Jessica are coming with me to New Braunfels." Ray was more realistic when he said, "do you think you would be happy living in the countryside of a small town. Jim said, "we have no urge to go back to Tulsa as we have already said. Ed added, "we love the Texas heat and cannot stand the Oregon winters. We are ready to move." "Then let's talk about wages and benefits."

Elle added, "since we already own a gun-shop, we are aware of values that workers appreciate. So let's start by saying that we will work 8 hours a day five days a week, with work every other Saturday at time- and-a-half." Ray took over, "the going minimum wage is still $2.50 a day for mill workers. We are prepared to offer you $5 a day with a dollar a day raise in six months, if you choose to stay. Lumberjacks and other mill workers will have their own pay scale and work hours."

Elle added, "you will each get your own home to live in free of charge for the next six months. If you choose to stay with us, we will negotiate a fair rent at that time." Ray then mentioned benefits. "We include medical, accidental, and maternity insurance. We will shut the plant down during the week of July 4th and the week between Xmas and New Years'—meaning two weeks of paid vacation. Short term disability for any condition at full pay—and that includes six weeks of maternity leave. Since we will be working with saws, an accidental loss of limb will pay $1,000 and an eye will pay $2,000, as long as you are wearing safety glasses. The downside, anyone triggering a spontaneous flash burn will be fined $50—with or without an excuse!" Much laughter followed.

Sue and Jessica had held their breath for so long that they broke out crying. It was Ed that said, "looks like you just hired four trained workers, heh?" Jim added, "well almost trained. Thank you and we won't let you down."

***

CHAPTER 8

Start-up Woes

The third week was following the routine. The mornings continued with Byron presenting two subjects and the afternoons were hands-on experience. Now Byron was introducing problems in the mill that had to be resolved. The weekly subjects included: the edging saw, the chipper, the water supply, the planer, the elevated roller rails, fixed or rotating jobs, and marketing the finished product.

That morning, Byron chose to speak on the edging saw. "This is a modern addition. In the old days, this process was done with the main circular saw and was way too time consuming. This saw is a ripping saw with guides that will rip off two-inch batten, one-inch stickers, and left over bark. It is a two-man job. The leader makes the determination as to which guide to use depending on the piece he wanted to obtain. He then guides the 1-inch boards into the saw as the assistant is on the receiving end. As the board is being sawed, the top rollers keep the board pressed down against the guides—thus producing straight boards. The assistant is also responsible for using the crosscut saw to cut off 4-foot stickers and place the excess into the waste bin destined for the chipper. Once the board is processed, the assistant places the pieces onto the rollers heading to the drying shed. Any questions?" Jim spoke up, "I find that deciding whether to make 2-inch batten or stickers is always a dilemma." "Well look at it this way, each 8 or 10-inch board needs one batten and the need will forever continue. Stickers are a different matter. The first year of operation will require a massive number of stickers—but can be reused from year to year. So next year you will only be making replacement or drying shed expansion stickers."

After the coffee break Byron addressed the woodchipper. "This is another modern addition and you might wonder why. Well it is because the ½-3/4-inch chips are the most efficient fuel for the boiler and the easiest to use. Since it is the product of any waste wood or bark, it provides a quick and hot fire. Besides, there is very little market for woodchips compared to the strong demand for sawdust from ranchers, dairy farms, and chicken coops. It is up to the worker who feeds this unit to gather all the waste wood produced by the crosscut and edging saws. Technically it consists of a flat wheel with four-inch elevated blades and four upright splitting blades. That way, the ½-3/4-inch chips can slip under the elevated blades. In reality, the 500 rpms of the saws are the same rpms used in the chipper. Some plants call it the 'HOG' since whatever you dump in simply disappears into the woodchip pile."

Jessica added, "I like this job since I am a clean freak and love to keep the worksite clean." Sue even added, "and I love the boiler/steam generator because I find it easy loading woodchips and watching functioning dials and monitors."

With time left, Byron saw the ground was treaded on. "That brings up the subject again of fixed jobs versus rotating jobs. We could battle the pros and cons all day and get nowhere because both methods are good and bad. Ed, what job do you enjoy the most?" "I like the master crosscut saw that cuts two-foot slabs and other assorted cuts." "So there, with Jim on the edging saw and Ray and Elle on the master saw/supervisor job, then I would say that the six major jobs have already been assigned. The remainder of the workers will become assistants or yard personnel. And let me add my two-cents-worth—in no time you will have six trained workers to handle your new sawmill plus a part-time saw sharpener."

*

The afternoon was uneventful and at 4PM Sue shocked everyone by popping off the emergency relief valve. The released steam triggered the plant whistle as the plant shut down when the valve to the steam engine was closed. As a response, everyone came to see why Sue had shut down the plant. Sue never said a word as Byron pointed to the psi valve apparently stuck at 100 psi. To give Sue her due accolade, Byron said, "very good Sue, now why don't you explain why you did what you did/"

"When I noticed that the psi had dropped from 125 to 100 I responded by adding more woodchips. But instead of the dial climbing back to 125 psi it stayed fixed at 100. So to prevent the riveted boiler from blowing up and causing injuries or deaths, I popped off the release valve." There was a long pause as Byron broke the silence by starting to clap his hands together. In no time, Sue was smothered in embraces and kisses. Byron only added, "never second guess the steam plant operators. Their decision to act or not to act is final."

The next day, Byron spoke on planers. "My first and final words mean the same—DON'T DO IT. If you are thinking of adding a planer sometime in the future, there are facts you need to know. This machine is massive and will require a shed twice the size of this sawmill shed. It takes several men to operate it including a mechanical engineer and a resident blade sharpener. There is no money in operating one to service your own sawmill plant—**unless it is demanded by your customers**. Your job is to make the best one-inch boards and to sell them to planing factories located in the big cities."

After the coffee break, he added elevated rollers. "The system of rollers is 30 inches off the floor. That makes it easy to work without straining your back, and brings the logs to the same level as the main carriage as well as the edging, crosscut, chipper, and drying shed. The only heavy lifting is done by the yard tractor."

Halfway thru the afternoon, Elle noticed that the circular saw was slowing down and was not maintaining 500 rpms. She moved the paper pulley to the zero position on the revolving disk and locked the clutch in place with the extra padlock for security. Realizing that the paper pulley was worn down, she placed the revolving plate to the off position and with Ray's help changed the paper pulley. The entire down time was a half hour and preventive maintenance was seen as a time saving measure.

The third week went by without any more mishaps. On Monday of the third week, Byron addressed the issue of marketing. "It does not matter how great a product you can make, if you don't have buyers, you are bankrupt. So let's work on how you can peddle your product. There is no doubt that living in New Braunfels is not the 'LOCATON-LOCATION-LOCATION.' So how will you sell your lumber. Keep in mind that a two-bedroom house will take 7,000 board feet, a two-story house will take 11,000 board feet, and a 30-stall horse barn will take 12,000 board feet. So how many of those will be built in your community each year. I'd say 10% of what your sawmill can put out in one year. So you have to market your lumber out of town. How do you achieve this. I'll take your suggestions and then I will give you mine. So who is first?"

Ray—"We have to advertise in the neighboring towns and cities. San Marcos is 15 miles east, Austin is 50 miles east, and San Antonio is 35 miles west." "Yes, and with the railroad they are really next door; as is Waco 150 miles east but by train is next door like Austin, heh?" "Good."

Elle—"We need to offer our lumber at a price lower than local mills. But insist that it is a cash price at point of loading at the sawmill shed." "Good."

Jim—"Send informative letters of introduction to well-known lumber yards in those four communities." "Also a good idea!"

Sue—"Offer that 13% discount for dimensional lumber." "Of course!"

Jessica—"Inform buyers that they have a choice of different firs, spruces, and pines—and list each species in the drying shed." "Good idea!"

Ed—"Also advertise sawdust, andslab-wood." "Why not?"

Byron paused and eventually said, "those are all good ideas, but they are fishing methods with ads and introductory letters. Why not have an open house and invite all those establishments to come and see your product. Make it an innovative event with food and beverages. That personal touch will sell loads of RR flatbed lumber. Also you have a major planing factory in your area—Waco. This factory will make a lot of tongue-and-groove boards used between San Antonio and Waco—with an estimated population of +- 75,000 people. I propose that your most popular 1-inch board will be the 1X6 board which planes down to ¾ X 5 ½ inch tongue-and-groove."

Ray interjected, "what about extending our reach to Houston, Dallas-Fort Worth, Texas itself, and even out of state?" "Possible but that means a salesman on the road, traveling on the train, all over Texas. Samples are a problem for salesmen, but letters praising your products from reputable sources, go a long way. Let me just summarize. Hire a marketing expert with a college degree and on the job experience, give them an endless budget, and be prepared to handle more than you can produce—that's the way to becoming a millionaire, heh?"

*

So the days went by, the Triplet's bond was getting stronger, and everyone felt comfortable while working all the sawmill jobs. It was the end of the fourth week as Byron finished his class on business management when President Winthrop entered with an entourage of his office workers. The President finally spoke, "Byron tells me that you have all passed the proficiency level in this trade. For this reason I am proud to distribute these certificates of completion and certified proficiency as a modern sawmill operator." After passing all ten certificates, President Winthrop congratulated them and informed them that they could stay another week in their student housing till their future venture was clear.

After spending Friday afternoon and most of Saturday at the pool, the Duo made arrangements to travel back to New Braunfels on Sunday morning. The Quad all needed to go back home to inform their families of their decision to move to West Texas. During the month all four Quad members had reiterated that there were no ties to keep them from moving hundreds of miles to an unknown small town and make a home and a living there. The final arrangements included a week or more for the Quad to make their goodbyes and pack their life's belongings as the Duo needed to get their gun-shop leadership organized and their sawmill operation shored up for their opening day.

The train left at 7AM and was scheduled to arrive in New Braunfels by noon. After an 8AM breakfast the Duo lingered in the dining car for coffee. Elle was somewhat somber when Ray asked, "are you sad that the month is over?" "Well I already miss Sue and Jessica, as well at that tantalizing hot shower. I swear you have found new ways to drive me berserk using that hot water nozzle." Ray did not answer but changed the subject. Eventually, he added, "we need to make a list of what we'll need to do once we are home." "Agree so let's start with the gun-shop!

1. Review the books.
2. Conduct private interviews with each worker.
3. Consider hiring a store manager or upgrading a worker to manager.
4. Change store hours, days off, and salaries."

When it came to the sawmill, the list included:

1. "Add fire, vandalism, and theft insurance for the two homes, barn, bunkhouse, sawmill, and the drying shed full with lumber.
2. Meet with the hired assistants, one tractor operator, and a team of seven lumberjacks. To outline their jobs, wages, work hours, and benefits.
3. Advertise to find a man to stack lumber in the drying shed.
4. Pick up small tools to include hand saws, shovels, brooms, pee-vees, log rollers, mechanical wrenches and misc. tools, leather gloves, safety glasses, earmuffs and ear inserts, axes, several bark spuds, 50 pounds of grease and 30 gallons of oil, grease and oil dispensers, and arrange for a regular gasoline delivery for the tractor.

5. Stock the shop office with desk, filing cabinet, typewriter, adding machine, ledgers, change box, and miscellaneous office paraphernalia.
6. Advertise to find a retired machine shop operator to be a part-time saw sharpener in the sharpening shed.
7. Notify Woody Industries to send their technician starting next week."

Realizing that these lists would take time to process, the Duo was pleased to know that they had +- 7 days to make it all happen. However today would be a special day—they needed to inspect their sawmill.

Enos was waiting at the railroad platform with the Duo's horse and buggy. After loading their crate and luggage, the Duo picked up some essential vittles and headed home. Walking into the house, the place was clean. Elle went straight for the water closet to pee, but instead screamed outload as she jumped into Ray's arms. "You wonderful man, I don't know how you managed that without my knowledge, but you will earn plenty of bonus points tonight." "Yes, well I want to use up my bonus points right where I earned them—the hot shower!"

After unpacking, they headed to the sawmill. First was a walk thru the main house, now with a hot shower, and then the new house, also with a shower. The water heater was a combination unit in a special shed between each house. The new house was also fully furnished.

Next was the sawmill. The Duo walked hand in hand as they stared at the complex. Multiple post and beam steel roofed sheds appeared on concrete pads. A sawmill shed, a massive drying lumber shed, a sawdust bin/shed, and a woodchip shed. Further checks revealed that the steam generator, edging saw, crosscut saws, woodchipper, office, and sharpening shed were all under the main sawmill shed's roof.

For the next hour, the Duo inspected the detailed sawing mechanism with total satisfaction. Their last inspection was the lumber yard. Every inch of the concrete slabs was covered with lumber precut to 8-12-16 feet and ready for the log cleaner. On their way out, they stopped to inspect the office and sharpening shed. Satisfied, they returned home only to find Durgin Stanton on their porch.

*

"Enos Ruttledge told me you were here and I was anxious to find out if you approved of our work?" Ray shook his hand and smiled. "I knew you could do it. That is a perfect job all around, so let's get some coffee and we'll settle up."

"With your generous deposit, the work on the sawmill is all covered. Now as far as lumber goes, I purchased everything from Austin's Goodwill Lumber. They refused payment and said they will settle with you after you start producing lumber. The house labor, steel roofing and plumbing expenses come to $1,000 and that is the exact amount you owe me. Again lumber settlement is pending but the house took 7,000 board feet and the sawmill took 16,000 board feet of mostly framing lumber." Elle wrote out a bank draft to Durgin and wrote in the bank book "Austin Goodwill is owed 23,000 board feet."

That night after a steak supper, the Duo enjoyed their hot shower. After reaching two long apogees, the Duo had to rush out of the shower **to avoid the cold water since the hot water tank was empty. After drying,** Ray said, "to avoid the cold water, we either perform two quickies, or a long slow agonizing one. heh?" "Or we get a bigger hot water tank and enjoy two long and slow agonizing ones"—again along with that impish smile.

Walking in the gun-shop, the reunion was warm and welcomed. After an hour of visiting socially, the Duo went to work. The books were well kept, sales averaged

$2,200 per week and profit was maintained at +- $1,500 for the four weeks. Afterwards, private interviews started.

Stella. "I have been working at the sales desk four hours a day from 10AM to 2PM. I am well paid, and ask for nothing. BUT, this business is too busy not to have a permanent working manager."

Amos. "I am fortunate to work from 10AM to 6PM. I help Roger or Archie whenever they ask especially if the front counter is not too busy and Stella is working. I hear a little bickering between workers and I suspect that would disappear if we had a resident working manager in control."

Roger. "I love managing the storage room. My only worry is when a train carload of guns or supplies arrives. The guns require two men to handle the long crates and Amos or Archie are just too busy to help me out. A working manager would solve my problem."

Archie. "There is plenty of work repairing broken firearms because of the non-durable gunmetal framework and parts. I am so busy that I don't dare stop to help Amos with sales, or Roger with unloading boxcars. As much as I hate the idea of having a shop manager, I guess we need one and I will not object to it because I want my coworkers happy."

Vickie. When Elle asked her how things were going, Vickie broke down and started crying. After she composed herself, she said, "I am literally overloaded with office work, to maintaining an inventory, to placing orders and paying for them, to payroll, to making bank deposits and many more duties that need done. I have had to bring work home and usually spend three hours catching up the day's work. I hate to ask, but I need an assistant or a working manager. Without some help, I will have to tell my man that I don't have time for him or have to quit my job."

Once done with the interviews, the Duo held a quick meeting. Ray started, "It is universal, we will hire a working manager with experience in gun-shops. You are all valued working employees and we wish to maintain that. So effective immediately this gun-shop is open five days a week from 9AM to 5PM on Mondays thru Fridays. Everyone working 8 hours will be paid $5 a day. Stella is half-time. Saturday 8-hour days start September 1st to Xmas and are at time-and-a-half wages. Everyone will maintain full benefits previously established. Is anyone objecting?" After a pause, it was 'thank you' across the board. On their way out, they walked to the telegraph office and sent an ad to all three local papers in Austin and six papers in San Antonio—all looking for an experienced manager who knows guns, has gun-shop experience, and has people skills.

*

After a quick coffee/chicken salad sandwich at Dixie's Diner, the Duo started working on the sawmill's "to do list." Their first stop was the Consolidated Insurance Company where protection was established based on a real-estate cost basis and value of finished products—progressive over the next year. They then went to the Town Hardware Store and established an account as well as arrange the delivery of the tools of the trade. Then to the office store to order the desk, filing cabinets, typewriter, an adding machine, and miscellaneous office items.

To the local gazette, they advertised for a retired machine shop operator to become a part-time saw sharpener. Then to the telegraph office to notify Woody Industries to send the installation technician for next week. After notifying the assistant sawmill workers of a meeting the next morning at the sawmill location, the Duo was glad to head home.

It was a quiet night at home and Ray was busy ministering to his voluptuous gal when there was a knock at the door. Feeling like they got caught, the Duo could barely get dressed in time to answer the door. "Hello, my name is Winn Dufield, I work for the Waco Electric Company. We will be laying out power poles and a line thru Austin to San Antonio. I stopped to ask you if you would want your own transformer to energize your house?" "Yes, of course." "That will require a $100 deposit and I will issue you your reservation. Now the last location I came to was a sawmill with two houses. I couldn't get close to the houses because of that massive brown dog. We could energize both houses, the sawmill office, a sharpening shed, and add power for overall lights. How do I reach the owners" "You have, will that be $100 or a $200 deposit? "Sorry but three locations mean three transformers or $300." Elle wrote the bank draft to cover all four locations. Before the company man left, he said, "the poles will be installed in one month, the transformers another month, and energizing the location entrance box another month. As a service to you, if you want an air conditioner for those houses, I would pay for them at the Town Hardware Store before the rush starts. Here are your four receipts and I hope it is not too late to finish what you were doing." Elle wasn't about to be outdone when she said, "not to worry, we are young and energetic and are good at picking up where we left off."

*

After a replenishing breakfast, the Duo reviewed the names of the assistant workers. Bass Winters— tractor operator, Ivan Inman unassigned, Bruno Terrill unassigned, Jude Yates unassigned, and Ollie Fulton unassigned. As the Duo arrived at the plant, the men were all waiting by the office. Ray welcomed the men and told them to roam around the mill and visit everything before they returned to the office for a meeting.

The meeting started with Elle asking if anyone had experience stacking lumber. Ivan spoke up and said, "that is what I've been doing in Austin for ten years and I am good at it." "Would you consider becoming our fulltime stacker?" "Why I would love to, thank you." It was Ollie who said, "we really cased this yard and you will need four assistants to help with the prepping and actual milling. With Ivan out, we are short one man. Would you consider hiring my brother Randolph, he wants out of the violent streets of Austin and settle down in a small town?" "Sure, have him come and see us." Ollie yells out to a man sitting on a rock beyond the yard. "Come and join us and see what your job will be."

After each assistant accepted a position Ray went over the $5 a day salary, the 8-hour workday, every other Saturday for time-and-a-half. and benefits. Once done with the workers, all were officially placed on the payroll while waiting for the mill to open. At noon, the Duo had lunch at the bunkhouse and then set up a meeting with the seven lumberjacks. After reviewing the wages, new hours, Saturday wages and benefits, the leader of the lumberjacks stood up to speak. "With room and board, we are very happy with those wages. However the July heat and bugs are unbearable in the forest and we always take the month of July off, but never take any other days off except Sundays." "Well your benefit package calls for a paid week off around July 4 and between Xmas and New Years'. So in that case we will pay your two weeks' vacation on July 1st and expect you back to work on August 1st."

*

Three days later, someone responded and requested an interview for the sharpening job and the manager's position. Eustache Gillingford was a 55-year-old retired machinist who had two reasons for applying for the job. "To my dismay, the Missus and I have run out of our savings and we need some part-time work to live. Also,

I don't have enough hobbies to keep me occupied and to make it worse, I cannot afford to pay for the few hobbies I have." When asked if he had experience sharpening saws he said, "the shop always did the local sharpening of anything from a paring knife to large industrial parts. Besides every saw comes with sharpening directions, hardened gauges, and the file grade to use. It is not a complicated science but rather a demanding job to focus and do a perfect job."

After more discussion, the Duo was comfortable with this man and offered him the job. Eustache was pleased to accept. When it came to wages or a salary, the Duo offered him an hourly wage of 75 cents an hour, a piecework fee for each sharpened saw, or part-time work five days a week. Eustache paused but was vigorous with his choice. "I need to get going in the morning so if I worked from 8AM to noon each day, I would have plenty of free time during the afternoons." The Duo was satisfied and offered him a daily wage of $2.50 or half of the regular workers $5 for an 8-hour day. To Eustache's surprise he was also given all the benefits that Stella had been awarded. As they terminated their visit, Ray asked, "how much do you owe your creditors?" "I owe Zeke Holiday $79, but without income, he is extending us more credit. Otherwise the house is paid for, is in great shape, and the property taxes are paid." Ray pulls out his billfold and hands Eustache $200. "Pay off Zeke's account, buy yourself some new work clothes, and go to the Town Hardware to sign-in to our account so you can pick up files and whatever else you may need to do the job. As of today you are on the payroll and we'll let you know when we start work! Welcome aboard!"

The next day a well-dressed man in his 40's appeared at the rail platform. The Duo was there holding a sign that said "gun-shop." "Hello, my name is Yale Stickney and I am the one who is applying for the managerial position." After introductions, the Trio went to Winnie's Diner for a late breakfast.

Elle started by saying, "tell us about yourself, your family, your work history, and anything else you think is important to get this job?" "I am 42 years old, a college graduate in business management, have a beautiful loving wife, three great kids ages 5, 4, and 2, and we need to get out of Austin." "Why?" "Because we live in a violent neighborhood and we will not send our children to the local school, and at $4 for a 10-hour day, it is hard to make a living and pay a mortgage." "I agree!" "As far as my work history, I have been a working manager. I take care of all office matters, keep an inventory, make orders, pay all the bills, work in the shop repairing guns, help the stock man unloading rail cars, and when needed, I work the sales desk. Plus if anyone is sick, I am the shop replacement." "But where is the owner?" "It is a widow who lives in Dallas and all she cares about is her monthly draft. No workers get any benefits for her approach is "either you work or there is no pay."

Once the food arrived, the interview stopped. While lingering over coffee, Ray went thru the new working hours, benefits, and emphasized the extra pay on Saturdays. Afterwards, without mentioning wages or a salary, the Duo brought him to the gun-shop for a tour and meeting the workers.

Upon entry, Yale had a smile on his face. He was escorted around the front counter, Archie's shop, Vicky's office, Roger's storage center, and then he peered at the handgun display as well as walked thru the rifle section. He peered at the shelving full of hunting accessories. Once he visited with the entire staff, including Stella, the Trio sat in the closed-door office for a final assessment. "Well how do you like the shop and the workers?" "Love the shop's layout and your workers are all impressionable." "Would you be willing to be a working manager and help out where a need appears?" "Why, I wouldn't have it any other way." Then since the workers are all paid $5 a day, we would offer you $6 a day and time-and-a-half on Saturdays with full benefits. Since we have a sawmill to operate, we would visit with you every other Saturday morning for major issues, but you would have total control of the day-to-day business. For catastrophic issues, you can find us at the sawmill. So when can you start?" "As soon as I find housing for my family."

Ray looked at Elle and got the nod. "Well let's go buy you a house to live in." "But my house is worth $1,500 and I still have a $1,000 mortgage." "Then sell it and keep the $500 to start an account in the local bank. Elle and I will buy your house, and will give you free rent for six months. Let the Austin real-estate agent sell your house, just move your family here and go to work, heh?"

The last thing Ray did was to give Yale $200 in cash currency. "What is this for?" "For you to pay off creditors and pay for your move to town. Now let's go find you a house close to school and work." It took only an hour to find that perfect family house. When Elle asked if his wife would be happy here, he said, "Wilma will cry for a month and will be unusually demonstrative with her favors." Ray's last words were, "then let me tell you about safe sex, or you will be using the family maternity benefit, heh?"

The remainder of the week was quiet as the Duo was ready to start work but would not until the four other trained workers were present.

***

CHAPTER 9

Full Operation

Days went by and the Duo was chomping at the bit to start that steam boiler and get the mill fired up. Each day, their anxiety grew till finally Elle said, "you know that we never arranged to cover their moving expenses like we just did with Yale. Do you think that is why they are not here yet?" "No dear, I had talked to the guys and they both said they had enough funds left for the trip back home and then the move to New Braunfels. Besides, we have their handshake on the deal. Let's not forget that one couple is from Tulsa some 500 miles, as Albuquerque is also 700 miles to town. And let's not forget that Sue and Jessica are like appendages tied to each of your hips, so stop worrying!" "I am really not worrying, I just miss them, heh?"

It was Friday night after supper that a telegraph messenger arrived with an emergency gram. Ray read it, gave the messenger 50 cents, and said there was no answer. Elle read it and repeated, "Jim and Jessica will be here at 9AM tomorrow."

That night Elle could not sleep. Coupling one way or another three times did not help and she managed to be up preparing breakfast at 6AM. When they arrived at the rail terminal at 8:30, Elle started fidgeting and never stopped till she saw Jessica step off the train. The reunion was impressive. Both gals hugged and cried uncontrollably. It was Jim who said, "there is no doubt that a happy woman assures a happy and contented life."

With their luggage in the buggy, the couple headed to Enos's livery. There the Duo purchased a harnessed horse and a two-seater buggy with a rear cargo area. Elle said, "this is half of your housewarming gift. Transferring the luggage to their new transportation, the couples stopped at Zeke Holiday's store to load up on vittles and start a credit account. The last thing that Ray did was hand Jim $200 as their belated sign-on bonus.

Taking the town road to the sawmill, Elle pointed to their private home as they passed by. A half mile later, they arrived at the impressive complex. Jim was impressed as he said, "wow, this place looks like a small village—two private houses, a huge barn, a nice bunkhouse, a chicken coop, a tool shed, and an obvious sawmill in the background."

Elle then said, "here are two houses, one is 10-years old and the other is new. Both are furnished. Head is the old and tail is the new." Jessica said, "head." "Head it is, welcome home. Let's show you around and put the vittles away." Jim and Jessica were thrilled at the living arrangements—as expected, finding a shower with hot water was the epitome of pleasant surprises.

The next thing was the sawmill tour. The Duo let their friends loose to check every station and shed. It took an hour for the two newbies to stop long enough to catch their breath. Jim said it best, "state-of-the-art mill, great location, great friends! Guess it don't get better than this, heh?"

That evening the two couples prepared a pork roast dinner in Jim and Jessica's new home. It was during dessert that the telegraph messenger arrived with an emergency gram. Ray handed it to Elle who said, "Ed and Sue will be here tomorrow at 8AM."

The process repeated itself and within three hours the Triplets were sitting in Ed and Sue's new house. Ed and Sue were totally amazed at the joint hot water heater and the associated shower. It was Elle who emphasized that the shower was absolutely needed to rinse the sawdust out of their hair and the sawdust odor off their bodies. Sue also added, "and great in promoting our sex lives, heh?"

Feeling that the two couples needed time to settle in and get familiar with the town businesses, the Duo said that the first day of work would be Wednesday. They would notify Eustache, and the Woody Enterprise technician of that exact date so the technician could be present at 7AM when Sue started the boiler for the first time.

*

Sue had a fueling problem since there was no sawdust, woodchips, or slab-wood. She had kindling, one bucket of sawdust, plenty of framing cut ends, and a few boards— all 24 inch long or less. With deftness, she had the psi gauge to 150 as she started the steam engine and let it idle at 100 psi. At 8AM, with a waiting staff, she pulled the start whistle and cranked up the steam engine to 125 psi as Ray's carriage was filled with an 8-foot long 30-inch Douglas Fir log. In no time, he had converted it into 8-foot-long full thickness 2-inch planks as Jim converted each plank into full thickness 2X4s. That one log had everyone working including the lumber stacker, the woodchipper and the crosscut saw operators. As a result of processing that one log, Sue now had fuel composed of sawdust, woodchips, and 24-inch slabs.

At 10AM, Ray and Elle changed jobs as Elle took the carriage controls. Her first log was a difficult one because one end was 12 inches inside the bark, and the small end was 6 inches in diameter inside the bark— and to complicate matters the log was 16 feet long. That meant that several 1-inch passes would need to be made till both ends matched. Each of these 1-inch-thick boards had plenty of bark on the edges. So Jim converted these into 1-inch stickers and cut them off 4 feet in length. Any residual went into the wheelbarrow destined for the woodchipper.

At noon, Sue sounded the whistle, the steam engine was turned off, and the boiler exhaust valve was left to maintain 75-80 psi while Sue had lunch with the other workers.

Abel, the Woody technician, had spent the morning checking all gears and pulleys to make sure that everything was working properly and secure to the frame. He tested every valve on the steam plant and was pleased to see things were working properly. He then announced that he would stay the day today and tomorrow, but would be gone by tomorrow evening if everything was still working properly.

During the lunch break, Eustache came to speak to the Duo. "I have checked the manuals for every saw in the plant. I know the approved sharpening technique and what files to use. Each saw has a guide/gauge for filing the different parts of each tooth as well as aligning each tooth. I have confirmed this with Abel. I have a list of files and other tools needed for sharpening saws and will pick them up at the Town Hardware store. I will be back in the morning. Assuming you don't hit an imbedded nail or rock stuck in the furrows, your saws will likely last according to the amount of dirt left in the furrows. So we'll see how long they will last."

The lunch break lasted 45 minutes as the last 15 minutes of the hour break was for the teams to lubricate their assigned sites while Sue refired the boiler to resume the operating pressure of 150 psi to start the steam engine and drain it of its condensation water. Then to let it idle a while so that by 1PM the plant was in full swing. The afternoon seemed to go well and at 4:30 Ray was in the drying shed taking an inventory of the board feet produced this first operational day. By 5PM, he had his final count of 20,000 mixed board feet with 65% framing lumber, 35% 1-inch boards, and enough 1-inch clean stickers to stack it all. As they were closing the plant, Elle asked, "what did you mean by clean stickers. Ivan won't use a sticker if it has any bark left on it because the bark will leak and stain the lumber—which buyers won't accept since carpenters will ask for a discount on the stained pieces!" "Wow, we really need to know the tricks of the trade, heh?" "Heck it's like any trade including love making!" "Oh yes, just like the tricks of the trade in our shower, heh?" "Of course!"

After a shower, some belated personal antics, and a fine supper of steak, baked potatoes, string beans, and a bread pudding, the Duo retired to their parlor. Ray was busy reading the local and national newspapers as Elle was busy on her Burroughs adding/multiplying machine. Once done she discussed her findings with Ray. "You said we had produced a strong 20,000 board feet of lumber today. Other than the fact that we will all become more efficient with time, let's assume some statistics with 20,000 board feet (BF) per 8-hour working day with 12 workers as we now have—and that includes you and me."

20,000 BF X 5 days = 100,000 BF per week plus
2 Saturdays per month = 40,000 BF = 10,000 BF weekly extras.
So the weekly production is really 110,000 BF per week.
Assuming we work 50 weeks a year (2 weeks for vacation)

50 X 110,000 BF = 5,500,000 BF per year.

The income from 5.5 million BF is (simplify to 5.0 million)

> 5,000,000 ÷1,000 BF X $35 per 1,000 BF = $175,000
>
> Plus add another $5,000 from selling sawdust, woodchips, and slab-wood for a grand total of $180,000.

Now let's move on to estimated expenses.

LABOR

7 lumberjacks at $5 a day for 8 hours = $30 X 7 X 50 weeks = $10,500

12 mill workers at $5 for 8 hours = $30 X 12 X 52 weeks = $18,720

Sharpener at $2.50 for 4 hours = $15 X 52 weeks = $780

Fulltime cookie & wrangler at $5 a day = $35 X 2 X 52 weeks = $3,640

> TOTAL LABOR $33,640.

OTHER EXPENSES—estimated

> Bunkhouse food, tractor gasoline, equipment parts, phone, small tools, oil, grease, sharpening files, replacement saws, horse and chicken feed._____$5,000

Miscellaneous EXPENSES_____$1,000

Depreciation and replacement_____$3,000

    TOTAL OTHER EXPENSES $9,000

Elle then said, "let's round off the labor to $34,000 and keep the estimated expenses at $9,000 and we are left with an estimated profit of $180,000 - $34,000 - $9,000 = $133,000 per year. Multiply that by eight years and you have +- $1 million."

After a long pause. Ray said, "that is more money than anyone deserves to earn." Elle retorted with "well we have to work for it and that is the way businesses work. Plus whom is to say that we don't start a profit-sharing plan to help our workers put money away for retirement. Many of our workers are already our friends, and by Xmas, I bet that most will be as well."

After another pause, Ray asked, "did you enjoy your day at the mill?" "I loved every minute of the day. There is something magical in seeing a piece of clean lumber fall off the log. Plus I am beginning to believe that the smell of sawdust is really the smell of money. How about you?" "I can't wait for morning to come and see the mill come alive." "Well at least we have each other and sleep to pass the time till the start whistle blows, heh?" "That is true for now, but I also want to live. We need personal hobbies, social hobbies, and nights out with our friends. For work cannot be the only thing we do, we need to live our lives and enjoy things while we are young and healthy, heh?" "I will never argue that point, but these things will happen in due time—as Sue and Jessica feel the same way."

*

The next morning during breakfast, Ray recalled something that Drummond Caswell had said the night they had come over to sell their woodlot. "I remember when Drummond said the woodlot contained 62 million BF of lumber. So if we can harvest 5 million BF a year of softwood lumber, that means we have at least 12 years to strip cut the 2,5000 acres of soft wood, and to leave all the hardwood oak for cabinet and general furniture grade lumber in the future when the demand matches the supply. For it is not good business today to turn 24-inch oak logs that are destined to be planks, boards, and 2-inch-square for poles and leggings, into firewood, heh?"

That day, Abel returned to Tulsa once he was satisfied that the plant was running smoothly. Also, the Duo realized that alternating their position between operating the main saw and supervisor position needed some modifications. Elle needed time to do office work and Ray would need time to make deposits and run errands. So if no one needed help, the Duo would use their supervisory spot for their side responsibilities. As an example, Friday night was payroll time. At 4PM sharp, the whistle blew as the lumberjacks, the cookie, the wrangler, and all ten mill workers gathered for their pay. Everyone looked forward to the time, not just for the money, but for the refreshments since Ray always managed to pick up a cold keg of beer for all to enjoy.

The first weekend was the off week. With Saturday off, the Duo decided to do their groceries Friday night. Being in a rush to get back in daylight, they postponed their usual cleansing shower and headed to town. Tying the buggy horse at Zeke's store, the Duo stepped to the boardwalk. They had not noticed a pair of useless bums sitting on the boardwalk bench. One spoke up and said, "hey shorty, look at the two woodchucks—one with a sissy sea-monster cap and a nice honey with full boobies. Ray hesitated and said, "apologize to my lady friend or else?" "Ha, ha, ha-ah, or else what; you smelly sawdust rat." Ray drew his handgun and the barrel caught Useless #1 right under the jaw as everyone heard a clear "crack." Useless #1 collapsed to the boardwalk as the Duo walked away.

Coming out with bags of groceries, Useless #1 was sitting on the bench and said, "heh, you broke my jaw, how about paying for Doc Sommer's fees ?" "Bubba, you are lucky I just didn't shoot one of your nuts off, for that is what you deserved. Now mark my words, if you ever address this lady in a derogatory fashion, I will shoot one of your nuts off, and that is not a threat, it is a promise, heh?"

*

Saturday morning, the Duo went to breakfast at Winnie's Diner. After steak and eggs as their rejuvenating energy, the Duo went to the gun-shop to see if Yale was adjusting with the workers and his new responsibilities. After pleasantries, the Trio moved to the office for a more private conversation. Ray started, "well what do you think of this store as a business?" "Beautiful store, well laid out, great workers, and despite a location with only 2,000 inhabitants, there is a great potential for increasing productivity and profits—especially with the onset of selling smokeless firearms with a winning Winchester Model 94 in 30-30."

Elle, not missing a trick, said, "what did you mean that there is a potential for increasing productivity and profits?" There was a significant pause as Yale said,

"Stella confided in me that you were hoping to take home the unearned income of $10,000 a year as non-working owners who have high assets invested in this business." "Yes, that is correct." "If I was able to generate a larger profit margin, what would you do with the extra profit?" Elle said, "as long as we don't have to add more assets into the business, we would do a profit-sharing with you and the workers so you can all start a retirement account—assuming you cover labor and all operating expenses." "Then let me propose this, I will pay you $833 the first of each month. As long as I have 'cart blanche' control of the money, I will generate a profit, over your unearned income by Xmas, or I will resign. Do we have a deal?" "Absolutely, and we'll meet on Xmas eve to review the books."

Saturday afternoon the Triplets gathered at the local range for a shooting event using Colt 1894 DA revolvers, and the Winchester Model 93 pump shotgun. All six members shot their hearts out using the 38 Long Colt and 12-gauge shotgun shells donated by Ray and Elle. As they were packing a man came over. "Hello, my name is Alva Zeller, and not to interfere, you are all fine shootists. You would do well to join our shooting club on road 7 north of town. There we shoot trap and revolver shooting on steel targets plus we have a plinking range up to 50 yards and a rifle sighting range at 100, 150, and 200 yards. Why don't you show up tomorrow at 1PM and watch a speed shooting competition. Maybe some of you might be interested in joining the club and or the shooting team. Here are six free entry passes. Hope to see you there, and by the way, I am president of the club and I go by the name of Al."

Saturday night, the Duo picked up the Quad and everyone got in the buggy to get to the town hall for dinner and dancing. It was clear that this would become the basic social event of the week. Both Sue and Jessica were following Elle's fashions with plenty of upper cleavage, a well outlined bum, and a hem just at the knee.

Sunday morning they lounged around the house till they got dressed for the 11 o'clock church service followed by lunch at Dixie's Diner. This Sunday, they stopped at their houses to dress in western jeans, summer blouses or shirts, cowboy hats and boots—as well as a six shooter on their hip. Stepping into the shooting range and club allowed many "rubber-neckers" to appreciate three attractive well-endowed females.

The Triplet watched a game of trap, but all agreed that it was too slow a game for them. Once the speed shooting started, The Triplet became alert. Everyone enjoyed the shooting of falling steel plates that were reset from the shooting line without going downrange. The most popular target was the Texas Star that needed an explanation on how to shoot it without causing it to spin out of control. It was again clear that to be competitive, the team would need to buy shooting accessories, practice ammo, and frequent sessions at the shooting range.

*

By the end of next week, Ray had ordered all the accessories for six speed shooting rigs, to include: speed loaders, holsters for loaders, clip on pouches for empties, a speed holster for the Model 92 DA revolvers, and a thousand rounds of 38 Long Colt ammo. Also, being their eighth day of mill operations, they already had +- 170,000 BF of green lumber milled, and with Saturday being their first weekend workday, they would add another +- 20,000 BF. That night, Ray pointed out that they could not afford to miss the late spring building season. They needed the trade to collect payroll funds as well as make room in the drying shed for drying wood since the shed itself would only hold 4.5 million BF. of lumber. So after supper, the Duo prepared an ad that offered newly harvested and milled lumber at $35 a thousand BF for full thickness rough sawn lumber. The ad was placed daily for two weeks in the town's Gazette—it also mentioned dimensional lumber at a 10% discount.

It was a week later that carpenters started arriving. They were curious about this dimensional lumber and most spent a long time in the drying shed inspecting all the different sizes produced. They were looking for bent, warped, rotten, bark staining, and spalted lumber. The biggest interest was the dimensional 2X4s and 2X6s. To the Duo's surprise, dimensional framing lumber was the popular order. Explaining to the buyers that dry lumber weighed over a ton per thousand BF, and more for green lumber, it was clear that a new house construction needing 7-12000 BF would need many loads when the local wagons only carried one ton.

As the workers arrived to load lumber it became clear that Ivan was way too busy to spend time sorting out the 1,000 BF. planned for each load and then having to help the driver load the lumber. So Ray offered a lateral transfer to the yard workers who were comfortable in selecting a 1,000 BF by themselves, help loading the wagon, and give a load stub for the office. One man jumped at the offer and even offered a job replacement referral for a good friend. Two days later, that man became a fulltime yard man.

All day, local carpenters showed up to pay for their orders. When either Elle or Ray was in the supervisor's position, they were the ones to go to the office to take orders and bank drafts, or there to accept cash from drivers that paid with paper currency for each load. After a week of this, the Duo was relaxing at home after their traditional therapeutic shower. Elle finally asked, "so what in blazes is spalted lumber?" "It is ruined lumber or a decorative alteration—depending how you look at it. So, if we leave a log in the hot sun all summer, at least 12 weeks, the fungi colonize and extract nutrients that leave dark dots and lines in the wood. Unless a customer specifically asks for it, the carpenters do not want any pieces in their wagons."

The next subject was about saw sharpening. Elle said, "Eustache has been keeping records and after weeks, he has a life expectancy of each saw. This is what he gave me as far as the number of days a saw lasts before it has to be sharpened and the teeth's outward angle restored to maintain a narrow kerf. It is all based on natural wear and the abrasive damage to the cutting edge from dirt or stones."

Master circular saw 2-3 days,   Edging saw 5 days.
Slab-wood crosscut 2 days   Sticker crosscut 7 days.

Chipper blades 2 days.

As June went by, the carpenters were busy working and the orders slowed down. Elle went to see the town clerk and paid to find out who the large lumber distributors were in San Antonio, Austin, and Waco. It was a week later that the clerk came down with a list—five in San Antonio, two in Austin and three in Waco. Elle spent several nights on her typewriter and prepared an introductory letter to all 10 wood distributors. It turned out to be a two-page communication that covered the type of softwood for sale and the going rate for fresh cut green lumber—especially framing rough sawn full thickness or dimensional lumber, seeing that the dry wood was still ten months away.

With the slow mail service, it was two weeks for a return correspondence. Four of the ten said that they would eventually make a trip to come and examine their product at their going rate, the other six were either more adventuresome or were desperate to fill their yards with lumber. Each of the six distributors had placed enough of an order for each to fill a flatbed rail car—which came to 5,000 BF of which 50% was green Douglas Fir or Spruce for framing, 25% were for rough sawn dimensional 2X4s and 2X6s, 10% were for 4-inch-wide boards for securing steel roofing to rafters, and 15% were for board and batten—all fresh green lumber. It was clear that these were orders to establish the quality of the lumber. As the Duo realized that only repeat orders would establish regular customers.

It took another two weeks for repeat orders to come in from the six wood distributors. This time it was for three flatbed cars or 15,000 BF per train per distributor. The railroad would send two men with heavy-duty wagons to haul the lumber and secure each stack to the flatbed car.

With local town carpenters and these six lumber distributors, the mill was able to fill the drying shed while maintaining a healthy income from green lumber to cover labor and expenses.

*

The months rolled by and several social events took hold. Every Tuesday night was card playing night at either one of three houses. Thursday was shooting practice at the steel plate range. Saturday off was luncheon and shopping for the three gals, and every Saturday night was dinner and dancing at the town hall. Sunday was church at 11 and dinner at the fancy Warton Hotel. Of course Sunday afternoon was competition shooting at the steel plate range. With the addition of Amos, Archie, and

Roger at the gun-shop, Team "R & E Guns & Milling" had a full 8-member team, ladies included, with one extra for each competition. The extra was chosen by the lowest card draw at each competition but kept ready in case one of their team was ill or disqualified.

The months rolled by and before anyone realized it, Xmas was upon them. The Duo had two events to schedule on Xmas Eve. In the morning they met with Yale. The meeting was held between the Duo, all the workers and Yale. Yale started, "I am proud to say that I won't be resigning. He opened the books and showed a $2,000 profit with all expenses, depreciation, labor, and the replacement account well-funded. Elle was first to speak, "as we promised, you are free to distribute these funds to you and your workers as profit sharing and we hope you will start a retirement account." With much applause Ray took over. "1894 is finally here and it is time to start selling smokeless firearms and convert this shop to a smokeless firearm store. It is time to stop buying new gunmetal rated black powder guns, and only deal in used black powder firearms. All your new firearms should be the smokeless type and I suspect the Winchester 1894 lever 30-30 will be your best seller."

Elle finished by asking Yale, "any idea how long it will take you to convert this shop to smokeless new firearms.?" "No idea, why don't we plan on meeting around the 4th of July to see how we are doing." "Fair enough, have a nice holiday and a good year next year."

*

The mill would shut down till January 2nd. At three o'clock the workers with their wives or significant others gathered in the Warton Hotels small lounge holding 50 or less guests. The mill was up to fifteen workers, along with the nine lumberjack staff, and all with their spouses and or significant others. As the workers arrived everyone was offered beer, wine, or a new Doctor Pepper soda from Waco along with cheese, cooked sausages, and crackers. The room was getting rowdy when Ray announced that supper was ready. The dinner special was a hind quarter of rare roast beef—sliced and served per each guest's preference. For non-rare to medium beef lovers, chicken and dumplings were a second choice. On each table were some baked potatoes and a vegetable assortment with rolls and butter. Lingering over apple pie with ice cream and coffee, the guests had ample time to let their meal settle down before the long anticipated first business meeting.

Ray started, "Elle and I have decided that a Xmas Eve yearly meeting will become a tradition." Applause followed. "To start with, your health, maternity, disability, loss of limb, and death benefits will be renewed for next year." More applause. Elle continued, "we will also continue your paid vacation in July and Xmas." Guffaws, whistles, and applause continued. "This year we have heard many times how work 'day after day' was a strain on people. So we are adding one new benefit. Every worker has three paid personal days off per year. All you have to do is add your name to the office calendar for the date you want as long as that date is not already taken. You wonder what kind of reason is acceptable. Well anything goes, if you want to go fishing, go hunting, have a birthday party, go shopping, repair something in the house, or just sleep the entire day away. If you need a paid day off, take it. For if you don't take it before next Xmas, you lose it, heh?" Much applause and lipped thank you.

Ray then surprised everyone by saying, "because of you, Elle and I made a lot of money. This is money beyond both our weekly salaries. It came from selling green lumber. You may not know this, but Elle and I believe in the 'trickledown effect.' If we make money, then you as our workers deserve a portion of that. So starting today, we had a choice to increase wages or start a profit-sharing system. We decided; everyone has a bank draft coming that is your share in profit-sharing. We hope you will use it to pay off bills, buy something you always wanted, but if you can, try to start a retirement account. Keep the amount private since it serves no one any purpose to gloat that your amount is higher than another worker. What you got is what we felt you deserve, heh?"

The Duo was watching as each worker opened their envelopes. It was uncanny as each realized that this was the most money they had ever held in their hands. Inside each envelope were $100 bills. The lumberjacks, Eustache, the cookie, and the wrangler all got five 'Ben Franklins,' The mill yard men got six, and each of the trained quad got eight. Everyone was obviously pleased and it was Eustache's wife who clearly showed a shocking relief from creditors.

As the meeting came to an end, it was clear that the next year would likely bring on new ideas and new marketing strategies, for by May they would have millions of BF of dry lumber to peddle or run out of drying space in the drying shed.

***

CHAPTER 10

The Sawmill's Open House

Xmas was an opportunity to enjoy a peaceful time with their close friends. The Duo prepared a Xmas celebration in their home and invited the Quad to attend. With spirit refreshments at 10, they had a classic noon dinner of turkey with all the fixings. Afterwards. sitting around a Douglas Fir tree, gifts were shared. Everyone got a Bulldog DA revolver with a shoulder holster as everyone also got a pocket derringer in 41 long colt. Since the Duo had both firearms, they both got a brand-new Winchester 1894 in 30-30. After playing a few hands of the new card game called "dirty board"—men against women of course; everyone went home when the men won three games in a row!!!!!!!! It was Jim who said, "boy, tonight our bed is going to be as dry as the Chihuahuan Desert." Ray added, "yeah, maybe next time we'll let them win a few games, heh?" Ed thought about it and said, "nah, Sue forgets all her troubles when I get her in the shower!"

The evening was the Duo's time to discuss issues. Sitting in their parlor with a fire in the fireplace, Ray blurted out, "I am not happy having to wait a year for lumber to dry. That is not an efficient way to do business. I think we need to do something about this. As it stands now we'll have dry wood available by May 1st but it will continue at a trickle till Xmas as we added more wood to dry each month." "In other words dry wood will be a progressive but slow availability. That may be satisfactory for local carpenters but it won't fly with lumber distributors. Since we have several of them as regular customers; you know they like full flatbed cars with 5,000 BF per car."

Elle paused, as she finally said, "I understand the problem, but what is a solution? Are you suggesting we build a second drying shed or expand the one we have since it only holds 4 million BF?" "I have thought about it and prefer another method. How much money do we have in the business account?" "After paying all labor, profit-sharing, and operational expenses, we still have $50,000—and as you used to say, more money than anyone deserves!" "Well, how about spending some of it to make more money?" "Sure, what do you have in mind?" **"Building a kiln that will hold 30,000 BF of green lumber and will dry it in 6 weeks instead of waiting a year, heh?"**

"Whoa, you've been reading behind my back, so spit it all out. Where did you get a book on kilns, when did you do your reading, and what have you learned?" "Well, drying wood is all about degree days. If you maintain the ambient temperature at 120-190° F. compared to room air, you hasten the process. Fresh softwoods have a moisture content of 30% or greater. After air drying for one year, the moisture is down to +- 15%. Six weeks of kiln drying, the moisture content will be down to +-12% and if left another two weeks will be down to +- 8%. Now that is efficiency in a timely fashion."

"Ok, so tell me what is required." "Here is a list of basics:

1. Electricity. Since we already have the poles and the transformer, I expect power will arrive within two weeks. We need power for fans in the mill and drying shed, but especially in the kiln to circulate the air and expel the moisture by roof exhaust fans.
2. Sticking and separating the lumber is still needed.

3. Each bundle of stickered lumber is limited to 500 BF since our tractor can only lift 1,000 pounds.

4. Width of each bundle is limited to 12 feet because of the width of the entrance doors.

5. Each stacked bundle is separated with 4X4 inch studs so the tractor forks can get under the bundles.

6. Pine boards are sappier and will likely take an extra week.

7. The kiln is built out of cement blocks, or cinder blocks as they are known. Each block has poured concrete for stability and air sealing. The walls tend to be 8 feet high and a steel roof has exhaust vents that are opened and closed via cables from the ground level. These louvered vents are how you control the ambient temperature of the kiln.

8. The source of heat is a wood/coal combination stove. Wood heat as slab-wood during the day and coal at nighttime.

9. A worker will need to watch the ambient temperature, control the louvers, and add slab-wood as needed. Since we now have six yard workers, I think we can assign the kiln job to one yard worker, as well as maintain some responsibilities on the main plant as well.

10. This kiln needs to be on a concrete slab continuous with the main plant and the drying shed, but far enough to not add heat to the plant area.

11. Once the wood is kiln dried, it is stored in a new open shed with a steel roof, where it will stay till loaded away.

12. Since there are advantages to kiln dried wood, we can easily add a few dollars to each 1,000 BF—say an extra $5 per 1,000 BF, heh?"

Elle was listening and picked up on Ray's last point. "So kindly tell me what those advantages are?" "Sure, here goes:

1. Time savings—for time is money!
2. Wood is less likely to deform or crack.
3. Kiln heat kills mold and fungus whose processes decrease wood value.
4. Dries off sticky resin to a hard clear powder.
5. Prevents future warping when wood equilibrates with ambient air moisture.
6. Kiln exposed wood is slightly stronger than air dried.
7. Lumber is much less susceptible to shrinkage if dried quickly in a kiln.

8. Because of daily humidity changes, the air-drying progress does not guarantee moisture content if less than a year. With a kiln, you can check the moisture content at least weekly with the moisture content gauge. That helps determine if the ambient temperature needs to be cranked up to speed up drying, or decreased it if it's drying too fast."

9. Besides, were we to have a functional kiln by spring, can you imagine what a great addition it could be if we have a 'mill open house' this springtime?"

"So that is your ulterior motive. Anyways, step back and tell me how this moisture content gauge works." "There are two pins that are inserted in the wood. A battery powered current flows between the two pins and the amount of current flow resistance indicates the moisture content. I admit that the exact % of moisture is not accurate between say 10 and 15%, but the downward pattern of several boards is what the kiln operator watches, along with the number of weeks, and at what the average daily ambient temperature is."

"Well I am impressed. Sounds like we need to visit with Durgin Stanton and see what he can do for us. Now enough of this deep thinking and planning, let's get back to personal basics." "Yes well, speaking of wood, unless you let go of my 'woodie,' you are going to need more than air drying to clean up its result."

*

The next day, the Duo went to see Durgin. "What are you two up to spending a vacation day in my office?" "We need a kiln and hope you can build it for us." "I admit I have never built one, but I have the blueprints for one and I know we can build it." Stepping to his private office he came out with plans rolled up in a tubular pack. Stretching the print over the counter, all three were studying the design. Durgin said, "the first thing to decide is the width of the doors which depends on the lumber's maximum length." Ray said, "say 12 feet." "That means two sealing seven-foot doors for clearance." Ray then said, "it also includes some requirements depending on the board feet you plan to dry at one time." "Let's say 30,000 BF." "That would require:

1. Concrete poured footing.
2. Four-foot-high poured concrete.
3. Four-foot-cinder blocks sealed and filled with mortar.

4. Louvered roof fans.

5. Circulating fans.

6. Concrete floor.

7. 40X40 foot wide and long. Center posts every 13 feet.

8. Wood/coal stove to cover square footage (1,600 square feet).

9. Galvanized steel roof.

10. A handy coal bin for nighttime burning."

After a pause Ray said, "sounds about right. How much will that cost us if you also add another concrete platform from the drying shed, another shed for kiln dried lumber, subcontract the fans electrification, and have electric lights installed all over the plant?" "Well electrification is not cheap and concrete is even worse. Give me a half hour and I will give you an estimate." The Duo had just enough time to get a cup of coffee as they returned. "My estimate comes to +- $6,000 because of the concrete and expensive electrification. Anything beyond that, we will settle after the project is completed." As Elle was writing a bank draft, Ray asked, "when can you start, and how much time to complete the job?" "We'll start Jan 2nd and it will likely take a month because of compulsory drying times for concrete."

The Duo spent the rest of the week fishing, shooting practice, playing cards, and dancing. Before they knew it, their vacation was coming to an end. It was Friday evening at home when Elle said, "We'll be back at work in two days and I recall one of your off the cuff statements." "Oh, which one was that?" "The one when you said, 'how it would be nice if we had a kiln by the time we had our mill open house.' "So, are we having a spring mill open house?" "Yes, by then the quiet winter months will be choking us. A spring open house will give us time to organize a real innovative gathering of wood users and distributors from all over Texas. I didn't want to start working on this during our vacation, but we should probably start organizing things starting next week, heh?"

Elle was quiet, stood and walked to the kitchen. She came back with a butcher knife in hand. "What on earth are you doing with that thing?" "I am going to cut your pizzle off since it doesn't look like we'll have anytime to diddle much till the fourth of July—as I assume it will regrow by then, heh?"

It was a long winter. By February 1st, the kiln was done and was filled with 30,000 BF of mixed 8-foot board and batten, and equal amounts of 8-foot 2X4s. By March 15th, the moisture content was down to +- 12 %.

The kiln was emptied and all the bundles were stacked in the kiln dried shed. The kiln was refilled and fired up. The worker had become proficient in maintaining a steady temperature of 170° F during the day and 150° F during the night with the stove banked with coal.

*

All thru winter, the Duo spent many nights planning the event, preparing an addressed invitation list, and even preparing the Duo's joint welcoming speech. It took several updates but they came up with a workable schedule of events.

1. 8-9AM.   Registration/coffee/pastries   and welcoming words.
2. 9-10AM. Demo and Discussion of softwood species, including the milled appearance of sawn lumber.
   Jim—Douglas Fir
   Ed—Spruces. White, Colorado, and Red spruce.
   Jessica—Pines. Ponderosa, loblolly, and long leaf pine.
3. 10-12 Noon. Live demo of entire sawmill plant.
   Boiler/steam generator/steam engine--Sue Bark cleaner station—Ray.

Main circular saw—Elle as operator, Ray as guide.

Edging saw and crosscut sticker saw—Jim.

Crosscut slab-wood sawyer—Ed.

Woodchipper—Jessica.

Other moving parts, conveyor chains and elevated rollers—Ray

Sawdust bin and woodchip open shed—Elle.

Sharpening shed—Eustache.

Drying shed—Ivan.

4. Noon to 1PM. Menu: burgers or sweet Italian sausage on a bun, potato salad, coleslaw, coffee/soda, and molasses/raisin cookies.

5. 1-2PM. Kiln tour and discussion.

    Basic construction.

    Advantages of kiln dried wood.

    2-week-old kiln dried sample.

    Demonstration of moisture gauge.

6. 2-3PM. Lumber inspection in drying shed.

    Rough sawn framing lumber.

    Rough sawn dimensional lumber.

    Rough sawn pine boards.

7. 3-4PM. Question and answer session—open to all.

8. 4PM till done. Private office—will accept orders, payments, reservations, or contracts with a deposit.

*

Next on the "to do list" was obtaining a list of Texas cities with 5,000 people or more, and get addresses for large construction firms, lumber distributors, city lumber yards, plus local carpenters in town and in San Marcos and Austin—the neighboring communities. For this project, the town clerk was paid 50 cents for each address he could provide. It took a month, but the clerk found 110 addresses of which they hoped to attract at least 80 potential buyers.

Winnie took the contract to provide coffee and pastries as well as catering lunch for 140 people since many of the buyers would come with their spouses or a head worker. Winnie agreed to arrive with the salads, but would cook the sandwiches on large coal fired grills.

The chosen date was April 1st and the invitations would be sent out a month ahead of time because of the slow postal service. The invitation was prepared by the Duo and looked like this.

INVITATION

You are invited to the first Texas-wide,

LUMBER MILL OPEN HOUSE

Place: Route 4, one mile east of New Braunfels at the R&E sawmill

DATE: April 1, 1894. TIME: 8AM to 4+PM.

COST = Free

Amenities: Morning pastries, hot noon lunch, and coffee all day.

Overnight housing for a fee Warton Hotel, Martha's Boarding House, Mama Mia's Boarding House, Rusty Bucket Casino, and free camping on mill grounds. All fees are reduced 10 % if have an invitation card.

Schedule of events: hourly demonstrations starting at 9AM.

Tour of working plant from power plant to drying shed.

SPECIAL: Guided walk-in tour of working kiln.

Thorough examination of all our products.

Q & A session.

Opportunity to place orders, or sign reservation contracts.

NOTE: RSVP by telegram ASAP. Need to know if coming and how people in your party. Respectfully R & E Lumber

Winter went by. The cool days were ideal for operating the plant. Working hours were maintained with the use of electric lights and the air was kept fresh with fans circulating air and pushing sawing dust out of the mill. When March 1st came and all invitations went out, the Duo knew the die was cast. By the ides of March, the Duo received confirmations for 80 or so buyers and a total 125 attendees because of accompanying spouses, significant others, or head workers. The last two weeks were spent preparing workers to be capable of explaining their part in managing a specific work-station. The night before the event, Ray finally admitted that he was ready and could recite his welcoming words without giving away any special tips that the workers were planning to use.

*

It was April 1st, and people started arriving at 7AM to take care of their horses. Everyone with saddled horses or buggies were directed to the barn where the lumberjacks were there to tag and bring the horses to the pasture and park their buggies/wagons, or bring the tagged saddles in the barn. Then everyone walked to the registration desk and enjoyed coffee with choices of donuts, bear paws, fruit, or sugared pastries—with plenty of seconds and thirds. By 8:45 Sue blew the whistle and invited everyone to the podium for Ray's welcoming words.

Ray started the event with the pledge of allegiance: "I pledge allegiance to.....................liberty and justice for all." "Welcome everyone to the first Texas sawmill open house. If we provide a good show, we hope to sell tons of lumber." Much laughter and applause. By some standards we are a small plant with +- 15 plant workers and +- seven lumberjacks. But we will saw some 5.5 million BF of lumber this year." Elle could see people writing this down on their day's schedule.

"To start, we have our own 2,500-acre woodlot of 50- to 70-year-old mature lumber that is ready for harvest. I can attest to the fact that our logs do not sit in the yard for more than two weeks before they are processed and you will not find any spalted lumber in this plant." People again applauded.

We have three species of softwoods: Douglas Fir, Spruce, and Pine. The workers will elaborate on these later at the 9AM demos. For sale right now is all the green rough sawn framing lumber from 2X4s to 2X12s.

Our one-year air dried lumber will start being available by May 1st. Plus we just took out our first batch of 6 weeks kilned lumber —but we'll hold talk on that till we get to the kiln's tour, heh? Other than lumber we also sell woodchips and sawdust as will be mentioned on the tours. Finally, as we tour you thru the plant, keep in mind that quality is what we offer and at an affordable price. So let's step to the three wood demos."

"My Name is Jim and I will talk about Douglas Fir. This is the only fir in our woodlot. Usually fir is a soft and weak lumber, but the reverse is true. Douglas Fir is unusually strong and for this reason we have incorporated it into framing lumber. The wood coming off the log is light brown and there are touches of red and yellow between the growth rings. 2X4 and 2X6 are sawed as full thickness lumber or in dimensional lumber. All other framing lumber is sawed into full thickness lumber.

"My name is Ed and I will be discussing the spruces. Our woodlot has three varieties of spruce—White, Red, and Colorado Spruce. It is also a strong wood and will usually be made into framing lumber. If you are short of pine boards, spruce will also make nice tongue-and-groove but the knots are usually smaller than pine. The sawed lumber is creamy white with a tint of yellow. Pitch is common with spruces and air drying doesn't always dry the pitch so be careful, it can be tacky."

"My name is Jessica and I will be presenting our pine products. We have three varieties to include: Ponderosa Pine, Loblolly Pine, and Long Leaf Pine. Since we have plenty of spruce and Douglas Fir to make framing lumber; all our pine is made into 1-inch boards from 2-inch batten to 10 inch wide. Pitch is less of a problem than spruce. The sawed boards look white, the growth rings appear dark, and the large knots appear dark. It is the best boards to be planed into ¾ X 5 ½-inch tongue-and-groove."

Ray then brought the crowd to the boiler/steam generator. "For the next two hours we will demonstrate how we turn a log into our finished product. Starting at the power source is Sue, our fireman and gauge monitor." "Hello, my day starts after the plant operators lubricate working parts. I then fire the boiler with woodchips and slab-wood. When the psi reaches 125 psi, I drain the 45-horsepower steam engine of water. At 150 psi I start the steam engine by opening the steam valve. I then let the engine idle a bit but when the psi reaches 125, I blow the start whistle and the plant comes alive. All day, I keep the operating psi at 125 by maintaining a fire of again woodchips and slab-wood, and controlling blow-off valves." Several buyers said, "nice job Ma'am."

Ray then set the spectators so everyone could see the log cleaner in operation followed by the winch pulling the log to the main carriage ready to meet the master 48-inch circular saw. Ray announced, "this station is the heart of the sawmill. This is where the operator can save the sawmill a fortune if the log is properly evaluated into its max production before its first pass of the saw. Elle and I have worked long hours in refining our technique and that is why she works two 2-hour shifts each day, and I do the other two 2-hour shifts." Ray stopped talking and Elle converted an 8-foot long, 24-inch diameter log into a dozen 10-inch-wide boards, a pile of smaller assorted size boards, and a pile of odd size boards to make matching 2-inch batten on the edging saw. The entourage was impressed and gave Elle a raving applause as well as the ladies obvious pleasure in seeing a woman doing a man's job with ultimate finesse.

Next was the edging saw. "Again, my name is Jim and I operate this fine edging saw. Basically I place an odd size board into the chosen guides. Let's say a 5-inch board. Well we don't sell 5-inch-wide boards. The guides will place the saw at four inches. I push the 5-inch-board in the guides, the powered top rollers will pull the board into the saw and keep the top pressure up till the two pieces are picked up by the receiving worker. Voila, a 4-inch-wide board and a 1-inch sticker. The combinations are endless. Then the stickers are cut into 4-foot lengths and any waste wood is cut up into 4-foot lengths with the special crosscut saw. The waste wood is then placed into the wheelbarrow destined to the chipper whereas the finished boards are headed to the drying shed along the powered elevated rollers."

The next station was Jessica with the woodchipper. "This is an amazing machine. Some people call it a hog, since any wood dropped in this unit comes out as ½ inch thick by ¾ inch long chips—bark included. The mechanism consists of multiple upright 3-inch blades separated by ¾ inches followed by 4-inch flat blades at a ½ inch elevation. It is a safe chipper since the entrance chute is three feet long and a foot wide. In short, I collect all the wood waste and it is all converted into woodchips—half used in the boiler, and half sold as heating fuel. Plus it is my job to keep this entire plant clean and any sawdust or wood pieces left on the floors are swept up and added to the chipper.

"My name is Ed and I operate the main crosscut saw. I cut all slab-wood into 24-inch-long pieces, and stack them in these mobile racks. Half go to the boiler and half go to the woodshed as heating firewood for sale. I also cut other waste wood that is not usable to make stickers and they also get stacked with the slab-wood or placed in the waste wheelbarrow destined for the woodchipper—especially pieces of bark."

Ray spent a few minutes explaining how the chain conveyors worked and how the elevated powered rollers brought wood to the drying shed. He also explained the woodchip shed and the elevated sawdust bins. Eustache gave an amazingly enlightening discussion about how each saw had its own file number and hardened gauges for the cutting edges, the rakers, and the gullets. The most revealing feature was a gauge that determined if the teeth were too far bent out to widen the cutting kerf, or if the cutting tips were turned off center. Of course he had an instrument to correct both problems. With many compliments, it was clear that Eustache was proud of his post-retirement parttime job. The Duo could not believe how Eustache pulled out such charisma to keep 140 peoples' attention on such a non-stimulating subject!

"Last but not least, the last step is always stacking lumber into 500 BF bundles. Ivan, our master-stacker will present this station. "As you can see, every stack is of one type of lumber and its length. So here we have 10-inch boards into the 8-footers, then the 12-footers, and last the 16-footers. Over here we have the full thickness 2 X 4s in the same 8-12-16 foot lengths. And so the pattern continues. As you can see, the bundles are four feet wide with 4-foot stickers every +- 3 feet. So an 8-foot-long board will have four stickers—one at each end and two in the middle. The final stage is when a bundle reaches 500 BF, the tractor stacks it on top of the last bundle—to a maximum of four bundles high and each bundle separated by 4 X 4-inch beams so the tractor's forks can sneak below the bundle. Lastly, since we added electricity, we've added fans and the drying process is twice as fast—I am certain that the bosses will discuss this at a later date, heh?" After another raving applause, Ray announced the morning half of the event had come to an end. "We will take an hour break for lunch and will meet at 1PM at our new Kiln. May I suggest you try two new condiments. With your burgers try the new tomato red sauce called 'ketchup,' and with your sweet Italian sausage try the new yellow sauce called 'mustard.' Try both since there is plenty for seconds."

*

The lunch hour was for new tastes and plenty of social visiting. Many of the buyers were talking to the workers and it was clear that they were interested in knowing more about their jobs. At 1PM Sue blew the plant's whistle, caught many by surprise, and several of the ladies had to go visit the privy. When everyone gathered at the kiln, Elle took over. "A kiln is nothing but a big oven kept at 175 degrees F during the day and at 150 degrees F during nighttime. The moisture escapes thru ceiling fans, and wall fans continue circulating air throughout the air passages in the stacked bundles— from ground level to four bundles high. We have just processed our first 30,000 BF of pine boards and spruce 2X4s. They have been in the kiln for six weeks and the moisture content tested at 12%. Now keep in mind that air dried lumber over one year will test at best at 15% knowing that green cut softwoods run 30-35% moisture at the stump. Walk around and see what it feels like to be in an oven with fans blowing hot air."

After the walk thru, Elle said, "when Ray and I were considering building a kiln, we discussed the advantages, and I will now give you those eight advantages. 1….3….6….8. Only recently have I found out that kiln dried lumber can be stained immediately and does not require waiting another year like when using green lumber. Think of the positive benefit for a new house to be stained before the carpenters clean up and leave!"

After another pause, Elle added, "I am certain there are plenty of questions brewing. Please wait for the Q & A session. Before we move on, let me show you how a moisture gauge or meter works so you won't be doubting our readings. This meter works by inserting two pins into the wood. The attached battery produces a current between the two pins. The amount of current resistance between the two pins is an extrapolated reading of the moisture content. Since seeing is worth a thousand words, this is a freshly cut Ponderosa Pine board. Feel how wet it is, as she pauses. Elle applies the meter and the reading was 34%. Elle then asks someone to randomly pull out a board out of the kiln dried lumber. The applied meter read 12 %. After much praise, Elle said, "it is said that the human body is 98% water. Do we have a volunteer so I can stick these two pins in someone's bum to verify the % moisture?" A couple of jokesters dragged a laughing older man as someone said, "he volunteers!"

Elle then guided everyone to the drying shed. "Ok folks, it is 2PM and you have an hour. Take all the time you want. Pull out any piece you want to study but make sure you are all satisfied that you have seen the quality we can produce. Bring your questions to the Q & A session which will start in one hour in the lunch area with sitting arrangements."

Once everyone gathered at the podium, Ray opened the Q & A session by saying, "this is an open forum and any question goes as long as it applies to the business of milling and buying lumber. So whose first?"

1. "I can see that local people can simply arrive with a wagon and load up their order. For us who are hundreds of miles away, it is a real expensive hardship to get our order to the railroad yard. Any potential solution?" "Yes, Elle and I had foreseen the problem. For the past month we have negotiated with the railroad. Starting next week the east-west line will be building a rail extension to our drying shed. It involves a quarter mile of rails, two switches, a siderail at the plant, and a road crossing on Route 4. The railroad will leave a gasoline-powered loading unit on the grounds and will load your orders as part of the $10 freight fee. The two siderails will hold six flatbed cars or potentially a maximum load of 30,000 board feet." Much applause followed.

2. "Are you open year-round?" "Yes except the vacation week of July 4 and Xmas to New Years. The lumberjacks do not work the entire month of

July because of heat—but that allows us to catch up and clean the yard's backed-up inventory."

3. "Are you charging extra for kiln dried lumber? "Yes, $5 per 1,000 BF. That doesn't even cover for the labor involved in feeding the wood stove. What it does is provide a service to our customers who need dry wood today, and not a year from now."

4. "I am surprised that you don't negotiate a special price for large orders say one million BF." Elle took over. "First of all, today we will not accept any order over 250,000 BF and reservations next year will be maxed out at 400,000 BF. The reason being that we only have two million BF available today and we want to supply as many customers as possible compared to selling everything to one large corporation. It is not wise to put all our eggs in one basket, heh?"

5. "When are you going to add hardwood lumber. Furniture makers need 2 or 3-inch 'square' for legs and backings, 1-inch boards, and 2-inch planking for tables?" "We have plenty of live oak trees and we probably could start next winter when there is snow on the ground to prevent dirt from imbedding in the bark and ruining our saws."

6. "If we don't need lumber this year, do we need to make a deposit for next spring's order?" "Yes, to reserve a specific order you need to make a 25% cash deposit today. If you cancel, we will keep 5%. We are not in business to shaft our customers, but we cannot stay in business with haphazard and speculative cancellations."

7. "Do you have any idea how much the railroad will charge for a flatbed full of lumber?" "Yes, I have the rates. Each flatbed holds 5 tons or 5,000 BF of two bundles high of stacked and rope-tied lumber. The cost per flatbed, including loading and unloading is $10 per flatbed anywhere in Texas. Now that is one heck of a deal." Many whistles and applause.

8. "Will you sell us partially dried lumber?" "Of course and we will label each packet when it was placed in the drying shed—but the same price as one-year dried lumber or green lumber."

9. "Other than your stored 4-million BF, what are you charging for fresh milled lumber this year and what is your monthly production rate?" "The price is still $35 per 1,000 BF and we average 110,000 BF a week."

10. Ray took over. "Why are you bothering to kiln dry 2X4s or 2X6s?" "Because of framing for inside partition walls. That is one place you do not want bowing or warping."

11. "I have been buying lumber from local sawmills for years where saw marks are the standard. How do you manage to have lumber without saw marks?" "Because of our sharpening expert and the fact that when a board shows the first saw mark, the circular saw is stopped and changed."

12. "There is no bark left on any stickers or any product in the drying shed. How can you manage that?" "We can achieve that by not allowing any board to be stacked with bark. We have an edging saw and a chipper that will take care of the problem."

13. "I have visited many sawmills but never seen a 45-horsepower steam engine when 25 horsepower is the standard. Why?" "This sawmill has many extras that use up power such as: the edging saw, powered rollers, two chain conveyors, and a power-hungry chipper."

14. "We noticed fans in the drying shed. Is this innovative and do they cut down on drying time?" "Yes, it is innovative. We have had fans now for 8

weeks. Ivan has been moisture testing the lumber each week. His results are showing a clear pattern of hastened drying. We hope we might be able to cut down drying time from 12 to 9 months. But the jury is not out yet to be certain. If successful, you will all be informed!"

15. "Are you going to electrify your entire plant and get rid of the wood fired steam generator?" "I am certain that eventually, with different power phases, that the plant will all be electric, but that is years away. For now, we are pleased to have electric lights, electric fans, and some electric powered hand tools."

16. "Kiln dried wood down to 12% moisture will still equilibrate with ambient humidity. So will this affect early wood staining if done before this equilibration which normally takes months." "From what professional house painters have told me. Oil based stain 'fixes' best to dry wood fibers down to 12% moisture. Once the stain is fixed, the equilibration to room or outside humidity will not affect the stain."

17. The group was quiet to suggest a near end till an older gentleman got up and said, "my next question depends on how many people are

planning to place orders today. So with a show of hands, how many of you are planning to place orders today?" Forty hands went up. "And how many of you are planning to reserve an order for next year's season?" Ten more hands went up. "There you go, how are you going to determine who is first, who is next to follow, when you run out of the 4+ million BF, or when you max out on the logs you plan to saw between now and next spring?" Ray smiled, gave the nod to Elle and said, "that seems like a tall order and we will make that our last question before we start the ordering. Since Elle, Sue, and Jessica have developed a failsafe system, I'll have Elle and the gals take over."

"Every potential buyer for this year and next will be given a ticket. The ticket is in two parts. The buyer gets one and the other is put in the hat. Both parts of the ticket have the same four-digit number." Sue then said, "when a ticket is drawn, the number is matched with the holder's number and that person is the first customer to enter the office to make his deal." Jessica then added, "depending on the deal, Sue and I will be keeping inventory of what sells and what is left over."

Elle then added, "and whoever is the first to place an order will also be the first to get loaded once the rails are in. In other words, if you are seventh to place an order, you will be seventh to be loaded irrelevant of the size of the six orders before you." Ray added, "any question on this proposed purchasing and reserving method?" With absolute silence, "then let us begin. Please step forward to get your ticket, and remember it also includes buyers who wish to reserve for later this season or next spring.

*

With 62 tickets handed out, the Duo knew they had a long business session ahead and would likely finish under electric lights. As Elle was ready to draw the first number, Ray added, "we will notify you once the 4 million BF have been sold. That will free some buyers who do not wish to wait for green lumber, kiln dry lumber, or reserve next years' batch."

Elle drew the first ticket as she yells out, "ticket #4119. A man yells out, "that's me!" Standing up was the man who had been offered as a volunteer to have the moisture meter test his body moisture content. The place erupted in laughter and applause as the older gent walked into the office with Ray and three beautiful women.

"My name is Waldo Crutchfield, I am 55 years old, I have never won anything, I have a construction company in Houston, and I am going to take advantage of being the first to order. I would like 200,000 BF of air-dried lumber dating from a year ago in this ratio; 70% of 8-10-inch boards and 2-inch batten to match, 20% 2X4s and 10% 2X6s. PLUS to reach my maximum 250,000 BF, I want 50,000 of green 2X4s, 2X6s, and 2X8s in a 60-30-10 ratio in favor of 2X4s." AND for next year I want the exact same order by April 1st." Elle did some computation and said, "that comes to $10,937.50--$8,750 this year and $2,187.50 deposit for next year." As Waldo handed a bank draft from a Houston Wells Fargo Bank, the gals were busy computing the inventory deductions.

The drawings continued. Three large lumber distributors placed large orders like Waldo Crutchfield did but the other orders were more moderate for both this year and the next. By 5PM and a total of 30 processed buyers, Ray announced that the 4 million BF were sold and that current green lumber, kiln lumber, and next years 4 million BF were still available. A few buyers took off as expected since they only wanted air dried lumber but the bulk of the other 20 buyers stayed to place future orders or current green lumber till winter arrived. It was 8PM when the last buyer placed a future's order of green mixed lumber even if told he would not get it till next spring.

With $200,000 in bank drafts and $30,000 in cash, the Duo, along with Jim and Ed, took a buggy ride to the local Wells Fargo Bank which fortunately was open till 9PM. At 8:45 four well-armed people entered to make the last deposit of the day.

***

CHAPTER 11

The Next Five Years

The evening after the open house found the Duo
totally exhausted. They had their usual mutual shower,
but no one felt frisky. After a reheated beef stew, the Duo
collapsed on their bed. Without the energy to undress out
of their sweats, the pair fell asleep. Come morning, the
two found the energy to wildly copulate. Realizing the
need to practice safe sex, Elle was fortunate to experience
a very prolonged and pleasant apogee. As usual, after her
release and recovery, Ray never went wanting with his
impish lover who would tease him into a near begging
situation before allowing his own relief. Each time Elle
did this, Ray would threaten to tease her to the edge and
leave her there; but seeing his voluptuous lover at near
apogee, he never made the threat come to pass.

After a traditional replenishing breakfast, Ray
asked if the tour or the selling session had revealed

some interesting facts. "Yes, and funny you should ask. One very observant buyer mentioned something that we always took for granted. We have developed our own sign language because we are near deaf with the ear plugs and muffs." "I agree, out of necessity, the workers need to communicate since they cannot just verbalize their directions. So we have signs for yes, no, start, stop, roll, lift, cut, strip, discard, save, and on and on. Plus we have our pointing index finger that also has great effect, heh?"

"What else did you discover?" "I don't know how to say this, but we have already taken deposits for 4 million BF on next years' lumber." "That is business security. Now what was the biggest disappointment expressed by the buyers?" "That's an easy one, not having our own planer to make four sided planed boards and tongue-and-groove." "Yeah, I heard many complaints about that. Customers want this type of wood finish. Finding a planer is not easy, often hundreds of miles away, very costly, and varied results." Elle added, "and I heard several buyers say they would gladly pay $50 a thousand BF if we had our own planer." "Yeah, well I am sure we'll hash this out again, but now is not the time with the railroad coming in and setting up the staff to make this work properly!"

"Anything else?" "One last thing, once we basically sold our drying shed's lumber we were left with 20,000

BF of 12-foot full thickness 2X10s and 2X12s. Why?" "Probably because they are too heavy and not much more support than 2X8s especially if they doubled them. So any suggestions of what we will do with that much lumber?" "To me, it is simple, bring the lumber back to the edging saw and let Jim convert the 2X10s to 2X4s and 2X6s with one pass of the saw. Plus convert the 2X12 to a 2X4 and a 2X8, or three 2X4s, whichever dimension we need the most!" "We can do, I will tell Jim about it and he can do some splitting when he has some spare moments waiting for the next board to split."

"Well that does it, starting Monday, we'll probably have the railroad construction to deal with, heh?" "Yes, the sooner the better!"

*

As scheduled, the railroad workers arrived with loads of rails, road crossing lumber, and two switches. Since they were working independently, the workers continued their usual routines. At the noon break, a well-dressed gentleman appeared at the office. "My name is Aloysius Abernathy, I am an 'interstate wood distributor' to surrounding states to include Nevada, New Mexico, Arizona, Louisiana, Missouri, Arkansas, and Kansas. I was here on Saturday and found your open house the best presentation I have ever experienced. I did not get a ticket because I was not about to compete with the Texas buyers. But I could not leave without bringing up a very important subject if you are to survive into the next five years till the 20th Century." "You have piqued our interest, but first we have to ask Jessica to operate the main saw till we are free. Then let's have some coffee and have a chat."

"I get all my rough lumber from western Colorado and Oklahoma. I then spend a fortune getting this lumber planed—to the point that there is no profit to make. I NEED PLANED BOARDS AND TONGUE-AND-GROOVE. So I am ready to invest into a planer, but I have no reliable place to operate it—other than this sawmill." "Well, that is a nice complement, but we haven't had time to think about this. First, we have to find a reliable manufacturer, find what structure we need to build, and where to find trained workers to operate it." "Stop right there, I have been researching this for almost a year and there is nothing I don't know about this subject. Please allow me to share my knowledge?" "Why, please enlighten us!"

"The gold standard in planers is the Woody Super Shaver from Tulsa. It is the most high-tech in our times and you know their quality since you have their sawmill. It is easy to operate for trained personnel but can be a nightmare as far as fine adjustments. With your professional sharpener, you would need one trained operator and one mechanical engineer to keep it maintained." "Well that's easier said than done!" "Not a problem, I know where there is such a team—a couple training at your old alma mater in Houston and graduating in a month. I have guaranteed them a place of employment and they are ready to come and visit your town and place of business."

"There was a pause as Ray said, "Woodie usually includes clear blueprints for the building that houses their machines and include a technician to install the machine." "I have those in my briefcase." "Really, well how is this powered, since our steam engine is at max." "A 40-horsepower gasoline engine, independent of the sawmill."

"Well, it is clear you know everything about this unit. Do you know how much this is going to cost us?" "$5,500 for the planer, $500 for four sets of extra planing knives with a mechanical sharpener, $1,500 for the planing/storage open shed, plus two assistant workers for your trained operators--$7,500 will put you in business. Say $8,000 to cover overruns." Elle laughed, "heck we can afford that, as long as we hire those two in Houston."

"No, no, no. I am going to give you the $8,000 interest free. You can pay me back over any length of time as long as you regularly send me some kiln dried planed 4-12-inch pine boards and 6-inch tongue-and-groove spruce or pine boards—at $50 a thousand BF." Ray said, "Sir, for the information you just gave us, you will have the boards as a regular customer and without a penny invested."

"Really, well then I have a second offer. Whenever you have a surplus, whatever it is, send it to me at my Fort Worth yard and I will pay for it ahead of delivery with a telegram voucher. I distributed 25 million BF of lumber last year, and I will take whatever you send me—your quality is unsurpassed. But to repeat, planed boards are best processed after being in the kiln for 6 weeks since splitting from long-term-air-drying ruins the finished product."

And so, Alloysius Abernathy left for Fort Worth, pleased to be assured he would be receiving planed boards. While at the railroad terminal he sent a telegram to an old friend, President Winthrop at the Houston College of Applied Sciences.

*

For the next two weeks, the Duo watched as the rails were laid down. At the same time, they spent many hours working with the new hire, Ronny Dunston, a mathematical whiz trained as a scaler and grader of lumber. It became clear that he could look at a 500 BF bundle, and after several notations and computations, would come up to an exact BF of lumber in the bundle. The results ranged from 450 BF to 550 BF. Seemingly somewhat insignificant, but it became significant with a 250,000 BF order. So for weeks, Ronny had been labeling each bundle the exact BF in red—painted over a stencil.

The day the gas-powered loader arrived, six flatbeds were loaded for the first buyer from the open house. The total BF came to 32,150 BF instead of the old system of assigning the standard 500 BF per bundle which would have yielded 30,000 BF on six flatbeds. It was obvious that the new system of scaling each packet had saved the mill some $70.

Once the six flatbeds were picked up, six more were left in place and loaded the same day Once the locomotive left, it pulled out a total of 12 flatbeds destined for one or several customers. On average, the railroad was able to accomplish a 12-flatbed sortie five days a week—or 300,000 BF a week to one or several customers. During busy railroad weeks, they still managed three sorties a week.

*

Once the rail system was organized, the Duo put all their efforts in making a planing operation come to fruition. First they placed a planer on hold, pending finding some qualified operators. Then The Duo had a serious discussion whether to find replacements for the number one position in the sawmill—operating the carriage and master saw. It was clear that both Ray and Ell had so much to do to manage the business that full-time replacements were needed. Jessica and Ed expressed an interest in the two positions whereas Sue and Jim were happy to stay on the steam generator and the edging saw. Once the decision was made to move Jessica and Ed up the ladder, the Duo decided to hire two new sawmill graduates and the two planing graduates that Abernathy had mentioned. So, the telegram went out to President Winthrop requesting his help in selecting such workers. The telegram also included salaries, housing, working hours, and benefits. Included in the telegram was a voucher to cover train tickets and traveling meals.

It was a week later that a telegram arrived from President Winthrop.

HELLO RAY AND ELLE STOP
NICE TO HEAR YOU ARE DOING WELL STOP
ALOYSIUS IS PROUD TO RECOMMEND YOU STOP
HAVE LOVELY COUPLES FOR YOU STOP
WORKERS READY TO MOVE TO NEW BRAUNFELS STOP
BOTH COUPLES WILL ARRIVE FRIDAY AM STOP
FOR A WEEKEND VISIT AND THEY NEED THE REST STOP
I KNOW YOU WILL BE IMPRESSED WITH THEM STOP
GOOD LUCK—WENDELL WINTHROP

With a week to plan, the Duo found time to make reservations at the Warton Hotel, breakfast and suppers in the hotel's restaurant, lunches at Winnie's or Dixie's diners, Saturday night at the town hall, and all-day Friday at the sawmill. Saturday would be the time to visit the town and see where they would use services.

The week went by quickly and Durgin worked up some prices on a new concrete platform, labor and steel roofing for the planing/storage shed, and two new houses with electric lights, a hot shower, and a kerosene furnace—of course the lumber for both projects came off the drying shed or kiln. On Friday, Jessica took the main saw as the Duo was at the train terminal by 8AM to greet the new potential workers.

*

Elle was walking the terminal platform with a placard on a stick that said, R & E Sawmill, Kiln, & Planer. The passenger cars were full as throngs of people came pouring out of the cars. The Duo never saw a beautiful young lady standing right next to Elle. "I am Samantha Dayton and this is my man, Royce Canfield, we are the planer students. Ray then had a tap on his shoulder as a young man said, "I am Bart Honeycutt and this is Faith Halleck, we are the sawmill students. After the Duo introduced themselves, the entourage walked two blocks to Dixie's Diner, as Ray had arranged for their luggage to be sent to Warton Hotel.

Waiting for their order of steak, home fries, eggs, coffee and toast, the six started talking about their days spent in Houston College. All agreed that two things were the best attractions, the swimming pool and the walk-in shower. Lingering over coffee, the guests were obviously at ease talking with the two young business owners.

Before leaving the diner, Elle said, "today, we will tour the sawmill and where the planer buildings will be. By 4PM we will bring you to the Warton Hotel where you will stay till Sunday morning. Tonight we will have a special welcoming dinner at the hotel and ask our two trained couples to join us—that's Jim, Jessica, Ed, and Sue. So shall we start with the tour, heh?"

Bart and Faith had a grin from ear to ear. "We love this mill and it is the same as we trained on. For Royce and Samantha's benefit, the tour guide acted as if they explained the sawmill to the general public—but added a few tidbits that only sawmill students would appreciate. To Bart and Faith's surprise, the school sawmill did not have a chipper, a drying shed, power rollers, or two chain conveyors to a woodchip shed and sawdust bins.

During the lunch hour, the students got introduced to the workers. Elle noticed that Faith and Samantha were occupying Sue and Jessica in intense discussions. Whereas Royce and Bart were clearly at ease with everyone and the quality of the working conditions. The afternoon was more of the same. Walking over the Kiln, the guests were exposed to the new building and got the chance to walk thru the heated oven. The last spot was the proposed site of the planer building. Royce studied the platform layout and the building blueprints.

When asked his opinion all he could say was, "what an incredible design, excellent! I would be honored to work in such a building with such a fine planing machine." It was clear that Samantha was pleased with her man's assessment.

On their way out of the plant, Sue and Jessica were waiting, in front of their homes, for the visitors to pass by. "Would you like to see the housing accommodations you would be living in?" "Sure." After another tour of both houses, Faith said, "hot water, walk in shower, central heat, electric lights, gas stove, why the only thing missing is an AC, heh?" As everyone started laughing.

Samantha looked confused as she said, "but I did not see where those housing units were located." Ray paused but said, "we will build them, next door to these two houses, once we have new trained workers to put in them."

Dropping the guests at the hotel, Elle said, "you have time to take a bath or shower, take a nap, and we will all meet at 6:30 in the restaurant."

*

At the restaurant each guest couple was separated by a resident couple so everyone could get familiar with each other. With wine and cold beer, everyone got talkative. It was Samantha who threw out the first surprising question. "So you have beautiful homes, good friends, and great coworkers, but what do you do other than living at home and working every day?" It was Jessica who said, "we work 40 hours a week and every other Saturday, but at time-and-a-half—which buys a lot of toys." Sue added, "we have hobbies and pastimes. We play dirty board cards every Tuesday night, we practice shooting on Thursday nights, we have a banquet and dance every Saturday night, and on our off Saturdays, the gals go to lunch and do some shopping after lunch. Elle also added, "we go to church on Sunday mornings and participate in the church's social events." Finally Ray added, and we all belong to a speed shooting team and compete every other Sunday afternoon." "Amidst all this, Ray and I enjoy some welcomed down time for just the two of us." Bold Samantha was so surprised that she just blurted out, "with schedules like that, when do you have time for sex?" Jim who never liked to be outdone quickly added, "a noon quickie in the sawdust bin!" It seemed that Jim spoke too loud since the entire restaurant broke out in laughter.

The menus were finally distributed. The special of the night was a 16 or 20-ounce prime rib with bone, a choice of salad or soup, choice of potato with three vegetables, fresh sourdough rolls, and dessert of carrot cake. Faith was somewhat taken back by the $3 price for the prime rib, but Sue quickly added, "don't worry, the business is paying the bill. It is another unlisted benefit, so enjoy and put away your guilt, or you will insult Ray and Elle."

At the Duo's urging, the men took the 20-ounce as the gals all took the 16-ounce. It was made clear to the waiter, that all bones were to go in a "doggie bag" for Browny and his two friends who were the nighttime guards in the plant. At the end of the meal, most everyone had trouble finishing the large carrot cake serving, but none were left untouched.

Lingering over coffee, more talk followed as everyone got comfortable. As they were all leaving, Elle said, "tomorrow morning we will drive you around town to introduce you to some merchants, the school, and the hospital. Tomorrow afternoon is your personal down time. Tomorrow night is dinner and dancing at the town hall since we all know you cannot go to Houston College without learning how to two-step and waltz, heh?" Sunday morning we will have a business meeting at the 9AM brunch since you are taking the train back to Houston at 2PM. The brunch is when it will be time to 'fish or cut bait' as the adage goes, heh?"

*

The visitors liked the layout of Main Street. They met Zeke and Mona Holiday at their general store, as well as President Willis at the bank, and the progressive principal of the elementary and high school. The hospital visit included a tour of the modern equipment and a visit with Doc Summers who assured them that he could interfere with a C-Section if the need arose and guaranteed them a safe hospital delivery with or without ether. When asked what the common cause of death during childbirth was, he assured Faith and Samantha that postpartum hemorrhage could usually be controlled with early uterus massage and breast feeding. If those methods failed, the hospital had an ample supply of "tincture of shepherd's purse, and a few other new drug concoctions."

After the tour, the Duo gave each student three gold double eagles worth $60. All four kept staring at the gold as Elle said, "the afternoon is free and I am certain you would all like to go shopping, but on a student's bank account, I am certain you would all spend the afternoon in your paid hotel rooms. Well, don't do it. Go out and buy whatever you need or want. We expect you to spend it all and have a good time. When we pick you up tonight to go dancing, we'll expect you to tell us what you bought!"

During the ham supper, the visitors confessed, the two gals both got their belated engagement rings, dressed up attire for dancing, and a personal derringer firearm. The guys bought a Webley Bulldog with a shoulder holster, and a speed DA revolver with all the accessories as well as 38 Long Colt ammo. Faith surprised everyone when she said, "the sales lady refused to charge us when she found out we were applying for a mill job. Of course, the owners were you and Ray. Well we told them that the money came from you, so the shop manager laughed and sold us the firearms at their cost." Samantha then handed Ray $12.50 as she said, "this is what is left over from our wonderful shopping spree. Thank you so much, that is something all of us will never forget"—as she kept rolling her engagement ring with a tear down her cheek.

When the band started, everyone got up to dance to their signature two-step tune. If was an evening of dancing, joking, and frolicking. Their table came to ten with the mill Quad included. During the evening Ray made an announcement of the two newly engaged guests at their table. During the last dance, Elle said, "I've had such a wonderful time entertaining these four students, and if they don't take the job, I will resign my status as social director!" "Not to worry, I think they are sold. Speaking of worry, I think you either have to stop rubbing my 'thing-a-ma-jig' by being so close, or we had better slowly make our way to our table—I think I am beginning to leak! heh?"

The next morning the Duo met the visitors in the hotel restaurant for a late brunch. It was a buffet so most started with coffee and a pastry. It was Elle who said, "Ray and I are at the point we know we need some help in the sawmill as well as operators for the new planing division. You have heard from President Winthrop what our hours will be, your salaries, free housing for six months. and work benefits. So what will it be, are you coming back in a month or not?"

There was a long pause as Royce said, "we met early this morning and I was asked to be the group's spokesperson. Just to be certain, are you really offering us $5 a day, time-and-a-half on Saturdays, 8-hour days, medical and obstetrical insurance, disability etc, three personal days off a year, and on Sam's and my personal level, complete control of the planer?" "Absolutely!" "Then on behalf of all of us, we would be honored and very happy to join your family of workers. One thing is certain, we will be loyal, will all give you 110%, and will be proud to wear the brand—as the saying goes." Hugs and handshakes went all around as Royce asked if signatures were needed. Ray said, "your word is all that is needed." After Elle finished writing, she handed out four bank drafts, each for $250. Everyone seemed to be asking the same question when Ray said, "this is your sign-on bonus. There is no doubt that your bank accounts are down to bare bottom. Well you need moving money, train fees, work clothing, and personals. Use what you need and when you arrive in a month buy vittles for your home until your first paycheck, and put a portion of your balance in the bank to open an account."

*

The next week Durgin was busy building a new concrete platform, a planing shed with an attached storage area, and two new houses adjacent to the first two. How he managed to do all that in a month was a mystery. The planer arrived in four pieces. The technician had two helpers to move the heavy four pieces into proper alignment. The Duo recalled the day when the technician started the 40-horsepower gas engine and then added a 12-inch-wide rough sawn board to the planer. Once introduced, the rollers controlled its speed of entry. Shavings were seen shooting into a box, as the new planed board was jettisoned to the rear rollers with all four sides perfectly planed. To demonstrate further, the tech guy made a few changes and a rough sawn 6-inch board was fed into the machine. In a short time a 5 ½ by ¾ inch tongue-and-groove finished board appeared. It was Elle who said, "the die is again cast, and the first load of six flatbed cars will go straight to Aloysius Abernathy in Fort Worth—and at $50 a thousand BF, heh?" "For sure!"

It was that evening after supper that the Duo was busy with roaming hands. They were supposedly celebrating the planer's installation, and roaming had led to poking and stroking when there was a knock at the door. Ray was grumbling and saying, "the last time that happened we ended up buying a 2,500-acre woodlot. To make that night worse, I didn't get any diddling, not even a……..as Elle was laughing so hard she had trouble getting her sweatpants on, even without undies. With near embarrassing scarlet faces, the door opened and a rarely seen neighbor was at the door—Obadiah Potts.

"Good evening folks, I considered seeing you at the plant, but when I showed up, Ray was gone and you were super busy on the master saw. By the way, that was a beautiful job how you converted the ugliest and most crooked 12-foot-long log into beautiful 12-foot 2X4s."

"Well, let's get some fresh coffee and you can tell us what lead to this visit."

Cradling a hot mug of coffee, Obadiah started. "I am 80 years old, have bad hips, have sold my house in town and heading to Austin where I have bought into an expensive rest home where they provide a bedroom, a parlor, a water closet, three meals a day, and a laundry service. I am free to go as I please, and if I get sick, they will take care of me. Well. I have no family, my wife has passed, and I need money to pay for that home. So, last July I took a walk in the woodlot you are harvesting and I liked what I saw. Your lumberjacks are not only harvesting the mature soft woods, but they are cutting hardwood saplings under two inches to make room for young softwood firs, spruces, and pines. I would like for whomever buys my woodlot to do the same with it so the next generation can have their own harvest."

Elle had heard enough and said, "so are we to presume that you are here to sell us your woodlot?" "Yes Miss Elle. If we can agree on a price, we could transfer the money and deed as quick as tomorrow morning at the town clerk's office. But being 80 years old, it might be wise to give me a bank draft tonight for a bill of sale marked paid in full, heh?" "We can do that, but how much do you want, what size is your lot, and what species of wood is on your lot?"

"My lot is four sections, 2,500 acres like the Caswell lot you purchased except there are no buildings on the lot. It has 85% softwoods with the same species as your lot, and 15% mature live oak trees. The woodlot is 50 years since the last harvest." "And your asking price?" "The same as you paid Drummond, $6 an acre." Elle got the nod from Ray as she wrote a bank draft for $15,000. Obadiah smiled and said, "that will take care of me till the end." Elle got on her typewriter, produced two copies of a bill of sale, marked paid in full, and deed pending.

*

It was later that evening, after recovering from their successful second attempt, that the Duo started planning. Ray said, "Ed and Jessica have had a month of self-training and work experience. They have become experts in using that carriage and getting the most out of that master saw. As far as us doing their jobs, well I am exhausted. I never realized these seeming simple jobs were so demanding. Of course the heat has been unbearable the past week and likely will continue in June and beyond. At least the fans have helped to circulate the air and dust out of the plant."

Elle then added, "speaking of fans, it was a good idea to add a few in all our houses. But what happened with the five air conditioners you ordered for our homes?" "Well to my surprise, the Main Street merchants got AC before private homes. That is why the gun-shop has several to keep the entire shop and storage area cool and dehumidified." "Any idea when we'll get ours?" "None whatsoever. I guess they will get here when they do, and this is nothing we can make happen like we did when we were living by the gun, or running a gun-shop, or operating a basic sawmill plant—when we still could make things happen." "I agree, now we have a kiln, a railroad loading center, and a planer that is ready to rock and roll as soon as Royce and Samantha get here." "Well, unless something drastic happens, we should have four new workers arrive any day now."

The new Quad arrived three days later and after taking one day to get settled in their new houses, they went to work. It was a productive month. Elle and Ray shadowed Bart and Faith for a week and then let them loose. Royce and Samantha got comfortable with the two assistants that Ray had hired. With the technician to shadow them, they started producing planed boards, planks for tabletops, and tongue-and-groove. As had been planned, they had 60,000 BF of kiln dried lumber to plane, and then would have to use air dried lumber till the batches came out of the oven every six weeks.

The experiment to plane air dried boards did not go well. Both ends were splitting and the splits were extending. The splitting occurred 20% of the time compared to kiln dried boards at 2%. It was Samantha who pointed out that the planer could now handle 40,000 BF a week, as production would increase with time. So for the planer to be kept at maximum production, more kiln space was needed. The original would double in size and the new one would also produce 60,000 BF. So the writing was on the wall. In came Durgin with his teams of carpenters and masons, and in four weeks, two mega 60,000 BF kilns were up and ready.

To everyone's surprise, Royce took over the job of watching over both kilns and the original kiln worker was brought back in the sawmill yard. Looking back, everyone agreed that proper functioning of both kilns was necessary to guarantee Royce and Samantha a job.

*

It was the 4th of July and the plant shut down. Royce continued adding firewood and monitoring the ambient air temperature and the moisture levels all thru the vacation. He refused extra pay feeling that the kiln's responsibility was part of his job and could not be shut down for a week.

The heat had been overpowering and there had been no rest with evening temperatures the same at night as in the day. It was a miracle when plumbers arrived and started installing air conditioners in all five houses. After the holiday celebration in town, everyone stayed in their air-conditioned homes till the vacation was over.

One night, at another inopportune time, the Duo had to uncouple to go answer a knock at the door. Ray was grumbling about another botched night out of four a month, and started for the door when Elle said, "you cannot answer the door with that bone on. Here, put your sweats on and sit down with the newspaper on your lap—and don't get up!"

There stood a sheepish Yale Stickney. "Sorry, I know that I disrupted something very private. I'll leave if you think it best?" "No, if you are here, we know it is important. So please come in and I'll put the coffee on." After some small talk, Ray said, "so what have you got on your mind?" "We've had some changes, Stella and Sonny are fully retired, we hired two new workers, and the original four, Amos, Archie, Roger, and Vickie want to own the shop, and so do I. We are hoping you are interested in selling."

There was total silence as Ray got up and started pacing the floor. Fortunately his tumescence had deflated and there were no tell-tale signs. Ray looked at Elle and asked that they have a private talk in the kitchen. Once out of earshot, Ray said, "is this something we should do?" "Ray, our heart is not in it, we are in love with our plant, that is where we are making our million, that is where our friends are, and that is where the miracle of making lumber occurs every day. I am so happy going to the plant every day that I am afraid the bubble will burst. Now I have said too much, so how about you?" "Oh gosh, I was beginning to think that I was the only childish one in this house. I feel the same way. The sawmill and all its ramifications is our future. Let's go sell a gun-shop."

"Yes, we are ready to sell. What are you offering. Well the bank has done a thorough inventory and has appraised the shop with all its contents at $25,000. The bank's board has given us a high credit rating and has approved a $20,000 loan since the income is so high. We need to find $5,000 and we also owe you a half year of your unearned income." "So you are short $10,000?" "Yes and no, but we have $8,000 in our bank account." Elle asked, "will you be able to pay your mortgage?"

"Oh yes, it is 25% of what we are paying you for your unearned income." "How are you distributing the voting shares?" "All four original workers are getting one voting share, and I as the manager get 5 voting shares—and keeping control of the business."

Elle gave Ray the nod as he said, "give us what is due--$5,000 of unearned income. That will leave $3,000 in the bank as operational funds. We will accept a selling price of $20,000 with a store credit of $2,000 for us or any of our mill workers." "Deal!"

*

It was six months later when the Xmas eve business meeting was held. It was a joyous day as the mill workers and the lumberjacks gathered at the Warton Hotel's restaurant for a private party. After several kegs and many wine bottles, the meal was served. A traditional turkey dinner. The meeting was short and to the point. Ray said, "It has been a very profitable year, we have made more money than we deserve, all your benefits are renewed, everyone is getting a dollar a day raise, and you all have a nice profit-sharing distribution coming. As usual keep your distribution private. Have a nice vacation and see you next year on January 2nd." The eight trained workers got $1,000 each and the yard workers and lumberjacks got $500 apiece. Plus the new Quad also had a signed deed to their house.

Two hours later, the Duo was discussing the meeting and the past year. It was Elle who said, "a few years ago Sheriff Dolan had called us Culminators. Well, no one can say we did not make this plant happen, heh?" "True, but I prefer to make private whoopie happen." "Well how about a twofer?" "Sure, but again at a very inopportune time, there was a knock at the front door!

***

The End

ABOUT THE AUTHOR

The author is a retired medical physician who, with his wife of 50+ years, spend their summers in Vermont and their winters in the Texas Rio Grande Valley.

Early in his retirement before 2016, he enjoyed his lifelong hobby of guns and shooting. He participated in the shooting sports to include Cowboy Action Shooting, long range black powder, USPSA, trap, and sporting clays. At the same time he wrote a book on shooting a big bore handgun, a desk reference on volume reloading, and two fictions on the cowboy shooting sports. Since 2016 he has become a prolific writer of western fiction circa 1870-1900—the Cowboy Era.

It was during the Covid pandemic, in a self-imposed quarantine, that he wrote a dozen books. A newly adopted writing genre covered three phases: a bounty hunter's life as a Paladin with his unique style of bringing outlaws to justice, a romantic encounter that changed his life, and the building of a lifelong enterprise that would support the couple's future when they hanged up their guns—as each enterprise is different from book to book.

Although three of his books have a sequel, the others are all a standalone publication. With a dozen books ready for publication in 2023, and to keep the subject matter varied, this author elects to publish them out of sequence.

I hope you enjoy reading my books, and if you do, please leave a comment on the seller's web site.

Richard M Beloin MD

AUTHOR'S PUBLICATIONS

Non fiction

Fiction in modern times

Western fiction (circa 1880-1900+)
(The Bounty Hunter/Entrepreneur series)

The Harrisons (sequel)—Book 6........(pandemic) ...2020

The Bodine Agency—Book 7.............(pandemic)...2020

The Bodines (sequel)—Book 8............(pandemic)...2020

The Bounty Hunting Sullivans—Book 9....(pandemic)...2020

Branch's Destiny—Book 10..............(pandemic) ...2020

Tate and Carla—Book 11..............(pandemic) ...2020

TEXAS LOAD—Book 12..............(pandemic) ...2021

TEXAS RELOAD(sequel)—Book 13....(pandemic)...2021

TEXAS BULLET—Book 14............(pandemic) ...2021

TEXAS SPORT(sequel)—Book 15.....(pandemic) ...2021

TEXAS ALLEVIATOR—Book 16.....(pandemic) ...2021

Western iction (circa 1873-1933)
(The Bounty Hunter, Romance
and entrepreneur series)

TEXAS GUNS—Book 1..............(pandemic) ...2021

TEXAS GUNS—2 (sequel) Book 2...(pandemic) ...2022

WAGON TRAIN TO IDAHO—Book 3.(pandemic) ...2022

DAKOTA AGENCY—Book 4.........(pandemic) ...2022

PRENTISS ARMS—Book 5.........(pandemic) 2022

COLORADO WORKS—Book 6...(post-pandemic) ...2022

COLORADIO RELOAD—Book 7....post-pandemic) ...2022

1880 WAGON TRAIN to California—Book 8.............
....(post-pandemic)2023

THE CULMINATORS—Book 9.....(post pandemic)...2023

Printed in the United States
by Baker & Taylor Publisher Services